Novel Romances

Angelo Thomas Crapanzano

Copyright © 2022 by Ayana Maria Dardaine

All rights reserved. This book or any portion thereof may not be reproduced or used in any manner whatsoever without the express written permission of the publisher except for the use of brief quotation in a book review.

ISBN 978-1-957956-69-5 (Paperback)
ISBN 978-1-957956-80-0 (Ebook)

Inquiries and Book Orders should be addressed to:

Leavitt Peak Press
17901 Pioneer Blvd Ste L #298, Artesia, California 90701
Phone #: 2092191548
email: info@leavittpeakpress.com

DEDICATION

I dedicate this book to all my brothers and sisters in Christ, andespecially the ones that are part of the West Hill Baptist Church.

Contents

ACKNOWLEDGEMENT

I wish to thank Richard Stiff for all the help he gave me in writing this novel. His notes and pictures of his trip to Hawaii were indispensible.I also thank him for doing a great job as Editor.

SURPRISED BY LOVE

Catherine was walking down from her bedroom to get some breakfast when she heard noise in one of the spare bedrooms. She went in to see what the noise was and was surprised that her dad was there fooling around in the closet.

"Dad," she said with surprise in her voice. "What are you doing up so early, and what are you doing in the closet?" Catherine's dad usual didn't get up until she had left for work. Since his wife passed away he did nothing all day. If it wasn't for the income from his fourthbook he would have no income. He had given up his job as an engineer and went as advisor on a part time bases. She was surprised to see him in that room. Since her mother died he was too grieved to go there. It was the room where her mother kept a lot of junk she wanted to save. Catherine had disposed all the extra dresses her mother kept there but she did touch the boxes of things she saved in the closet.

"I couldn't sleep so I thought I should get rid of some of the stuff your mother saved in the closet," answered her dad. "I got rid of a box of old paper articles she saved and many out dated coupons. This last box is full of magazines she saved."

"What," asked Catherine "is that one you are holding in your hand and keep staring at the cover?"

"It's very strange that your mother saved this one, replied her father. "It is about five years old and has a picture of a movie starthat I had very strong feeling for."

"You were in love with a movie star?"

"Well you wouldn't say that I was in love with her because I never met her," answered Tom. "But I had strong feeling for her."

"What was it about her that you liked?" asked Catherine. "I cansee that she is beautiful."

"It wasn't just her looks," answered her father. "She was gentle and so upbeat. She was very affectionate and her brown eyes smiled even when she was playing a serious scene. I loved her voice. She was so graceful in every action she took."

"Dad," she said with a silly grin on her face. "You are in love with a girl you never met."

"I just respect her that is all," answered her father. "She was so much like your mother. In fact that may be one of the factors that made me fall for your mother."

"Sure," said Catherine, with a smirk on her face. "I see how you are staring at her picture."

"So I like looking at her," said her father.

"Well I have to go," said Catherine. "Why don't you look inside and read about her. It might relieve some of that loving look I see in your eyes." Catherine went down to the kitchen to get some breakfast. She wasn't there more than a minute when she heard a loud yell from her father. She ran up the stairs taking two at a time. "Dad" she yelled what is wrong?"

"I can't believe that they would do something like this," he yelled. "This is crazy?"

"What are you talking about? You scared me half to death?" said Catherine.

"It's the pictures they have in the inside pages. It's got to be illegal," said her dad. "I don't understand why your mother kept this magazine. Why didn't she say something? Did she think I was cheating on her?"

He then showed the page with the picture he was talking about.

"That's a picture of you next to her," said Catherine almost to herself. Then turning the page she said, "And here you are hugging her in this picture. I thought you never met her."

"I never met her," responded her father. "It has to be my pictures or someone who looks identical to me." Catherine took a very close look at the picture.

"That has to be you," she said. "No one could look so much like you."

"These days they can do anything with photos. I don't understand why they wanted to use my pictures,"

"It might be that you look a lot like her husband and since he was dead they used yours," suggested Catherine.

"Without my knowledge, isn't that illegal?"

"Dad," responded Catherine,"So what are you going to do about it? Why don't you call the magazine? I'm sure they have a phone number in the magazine somewhere. I have to go dad, I'm already late." Catherine left and Tom sat there thinking about what he was going to do. He decided to call the magazine and find out what they would say about it. He found the phone number and called them.

"Hello," said a male voice, "how can I help you?"

"I want to speak to someone about an article that was written in your magazine on April 2012"

"That was five years ago," said the man. "We don't go back that far in answering questions on an article."

"Well you had better, said Tom. "What you did in that article is illegal."

"What article are you talking about?" asked the man now getting interested. "What is the problem?"

"It is the article about the life of actress Debra Lee," said Tom. "It has a picture of me in it and I did not even know about it, let alone approve of it."

"Are you talking about the Debra Lee the actress of several romantic movies of several years ago?"

"That's right," said Tom. Before he could say any more, the man continued.

"That is Fred's special article. He was wild when he wrote that article. He couldn't stop talking about her. Wait a minute and I'll get him. He could answer all your questions." Several minutes later a man came to the phone.

"I'm Fred," he said. "What is this about the article I wrote five years ago?"

"Where did you get the pictures of her," asked Tom? "I got them from her album. I saw her remove them." "Did she give you the pictures?"

"Yes she gave me the picture but after I used them, I mailed them back to her. If you are looking to get your hands on them, you have to contact her."

"Well you give me her address?"

"I can't," said Fred, "If I do that I would get in trouble with my boss."

"I was just reading the article and I noticed that my pictures where included in the article as her husband."

"That's not possible because her husband died several months before she would let me interview her. I would guess that you are alive."

"That's the point," said Tom. "What kind of photo trickery was done to get my picture with her?"

"You will have to ask her that question," said Fred. "She gave me those pictures right from her album."

"Tell you what I will do," suggested Tom. "I will do two things for that address. First I promise that no one will ever know that you gave me the address. Secondly I think that something strange is going on. I will go there and when I find out what is going on, I will give only you the exclusive story. What do you say?"

"That's a deal," said Fred and seconds later gave Tom the address.

That evening when Catherine got home, Tom was ready to discuss what action he should take. After diner Tom asked his daughter.

"I got the address of Debra Lee, but what do you think I should do? Should I write her a letter, or should I try to get her phone number and call her?"

"Where is her house located," asked Catherine?

"Her house is in South Haven, Indiana. It is just south east of gary, Indiana."

"I think you should go to see her and ask her person-ally about your picture," said Catherine with a smile on her face. "I'm sure you would like to see her anyway."

"That's a long drive," said Tom. "I think it would take four or five hours at least."

"So," said Catherine, "what do you have to do anyway that you can't put off for a few days. go tomorrow and get a room near her house so that you can freshen up when you go to see her. Besides you may have to go several times. She may be at work. She has to work to buy food and stuff."

"Are you serious or are you kidding," asked Tom?

"Dad I'm very serious. go. You need to get away anyway. go."

Tom couldn't make up his mind. It was after lunch that he decided to go. The trip was not too bad. It was all a great high way driving until he got to gary, Indiana. He got to South Haven about five thirty. He found a small motel and got a room. He freshened up and went to Debra's house. There was no one home as he expected. She must be at work he surmised. He went back to the motel and after diner about nine he returned to the house. The lights were all out. Again there was no one home. The next morning he decided to go early. It was about seven thirty when he got to the house. He was about to ring the doorbell when the door opened and a young girl was about to exit. Suddenly when she looked up and saw Tom she gave out a yell and started to pass out. The door kept her from falling backwards so she fell forward into Tom's arms. Tom picked her up and took her inside and laid her on the sofa just inside the room.

"I'm sorry I scared you,"said Tom as she seemed to be awakening. She suddenly looked at Tom and pushed herself up against the sofa as far as she could with a scared look on her face. "Daddy," she yelled. "Are you a ghost?"

"No," said Tom being as amazed at her question. "I am not your dad. I'm sorry if I have caused you a problem."

"Who are you?" asked the young lady, "and what are you doing here?"

"My name is Tom Corelli. I came here to find out why my picture is displayed with Debra Lee. Your calling me daddy answers some of my questions. Debra is apparently your mother, and I look a lot like your father."

"Who are you really," asked the young lady?

"That is a good question," responded Tom. "Let me go back to the beginning. I was born in Cleveland ohio. When I got married I moved to Fairlawn ohio. It is a suburb of Akron. It is better known as the Rubber City. my wife died about three years ago. She kept many of her things in the spare bedroom. I was too grieved to clean out the closet in that room. my daughter cleaned out the dresses in the closet but left the cardboard box alone. Yesterday I decided to clean out the closet. In a cardboard box I found several old magazines. one of them had a picture of Debra Lee on the cover. About ten years ago I saw most of her Tv movies. I had a crush on her, not just because she is beautiful but because of her upbeat personality. Anyway, I looked inside and was flabbergasted that she was pictured in two places with me. How and why was I pictured with her? You have answered that question. It wasn't me in those pictures. It was you father who I apparently look like. The question now is why I look so much like your father. There must be some sort of a relationship. Speaking of you mother, where is she?"

"My mother is in the hospital," said the young lady. "That is where I was going when I bumped into you."

"Is she oK?" asked Tom being concern more then he thought he would be.

"Yes," said the young lady. "She has a gallbladder problem. The doctor wants to operate but she is too depressed. I think he said that depression does something to her blood pressure."

"I'm sorry. I didn't mean to hold you up,"said Tom apologetically. "By the way what is your name?"

"My name is Janet."

"I believe that Lee is your mother's movie name. What is her real name?"

"Her full name, before she got married was Debra Lee Darden. "What is her and your last name today?"

"My full name is Janet Lena morello." Tom fell back in his chair and almost fell off. He was in a state of shock. He put his hand on his forehead and yelled,

"Dear Lord."

"Are you all right," asked Jan? "Is it something I said?"

"No," said John. "Please let me think awhile." Jan was surprised by Tom's reaction. She didn't have the slightest idea at what was going on. She however kept quiet. After several minutes Tom looked at Jan. "Are your grandparents, on your father's side, named Antonio and Lina morello?" Jan was shocked.

"How did you know that," she asked?

"Dear Lord, Let me think about this for a bit and perhaps I could figure this out." After a while he sat up and asked, "Do your grandparents live in Chicago?"

"Yes" said Jan. "What does this have anything to do with anything?"

"I think I may have some answers to some of our questions," answered Tom.

"I'm so confused I don't even know the questions," said Jan. "What triggered me is when you said that your last name was morello. You see my mother's maiden name is morello. I have an uncle who is named Antonio and is married to a Lina. But I was told that they live in northern Italy."

"I think that I'm following this a little," said Jan. "You are looking for a relationship."Tom shook his head up and down slightly and put his hand up to say wait a moment. Tom then went into deep thought. After several minutes he looked up with a smile.

"I think I have a possible answer," said Tom. "You see my mother had a reason to lie to me as to where they lived. She was obviously hiding something. That's why I never met Uncle Antonio or Aunt Lina. I remember one day when I found my mother was very sad. I hear her telling my father that Aunt Lina had a surgery and that she would never have a child. Here is what I think happened. my father and Uncle Joe bought a two family house in Cleveland before my father went back to Sicily and got married. They stayed there over a year. I suspect that they came back because my mother was pregnant. The airline does not have a flight to Cleveland. You have to go to Chicago and get a flight from there to Cleveland. I think that uncle

Antonio and Aunt Lina lived in Chicago. After my parents landed in Chicago, they of course went to visit my mother's brother. my mother must have known she was pregnant with twins. my mother is a very sensitive person. She also was new to America. I think she was concerned about raising one child let alone two. Somehow they must have talked her into giving her brother one of her twins. Knowing how sensitive my mother is I suspect that she never saw her first child. She let herself believe that she only had the one child, me. I further suspect that they had a midwife claim that she delivered me in Cleveland and gave me a birth certificate that states that. I believe my uncle did the same thing with you father. Also it is customary for Italians to name the first child after the grandfather on the father's side. my grandfather was named Joseph. The second child is named after the grandfather on the mother's side. my grandfather on my mother's side was Thomas. It all makes sense."

"Wow," said Jan. "That would explain why you look like my father."

"Get up and come here," said Tom to Jan. She complied not knowing what he had in mind. When she got near to Tom, he grabbed her and gave her a very affectionate hug.

"What," said Jan looking into Tom's eyes? Before she could say more he responded to the question he knew she wanted to ask.

"You're my niece," said Tom. "You're my brother's daughter. Can't I hug my lovely niece?"

"Sure, Uncle Tom," said Jan with a smile on her face. "You can hug me anytime you feel like."

"I think now we should go and see your mother," said Tom. "I think that she must be very worried by now. Do you want me to drive?"

"No," said Jan. "I can't stay long. I have to go to work. I work from one to nine every day."

"I would like to know more about you," said John. "Where do you work?"

"I am home from school for the summer. I am studying to be a nurse. Currently I'm working in a grocery store. I help in the meat department." They had just reached Jan's car, when she asked him the same question. "How about you, what do you do?"

"I graduated as an electronic engineer," responded Tom. "However, I am now working independently, providing computer software for financial departments. But most of the time I am an author. I have had six novels published to date."

"Wow, that is great," said Jan being impressed. "my uncle is a famous man." Tom smiled at her.

"I won't tell you the truth," said Tom. "I don't want to dissolution you."

"Well," said Jan. "You can never do that. Anyway just follow me to the hospital. It's only a ten minute drive."

When they got to the hospital parking lot Jan found a spot and parked her car. Tom found one about two cars away. Without any words Tom followed Jan into the hospital and using the elevator they preceded to the third floor. Jan walked down the aisle way until they got to the nurses quarters. Across from the nurses desk was a small table with four chairs and a sofa.

"Uncle Tom," said Jan, "Will you wait here. I think I have to prepare mom before she sees you. Just sit here and I'll come and get you when I have prepared her. Her room is just two rooms down on the left side of the aisle. By the way everyone knows her as Debbie"

When Jan walked into her mother hospital room, her mother yelled out.

"Where have you been? I was so worried about you. It's almost eleven. Don't you have to go to work?"

"Mom, just relax," said Jan trying to be as loving and gentle as she could be. "I have a very exciting thing to tell you. Just sit and let me explain." Jan started with the time she opened the door and saw Tom. She explained how he looks so much like dad. "mom you just can't believe it until you see him. We spent most of the morning trying to find a relationship. I think we found one, But I think you should hear it all from him."

"Where is he," asked her mother? "I can't believe he really looks like your dad."

"He is sitting in the waiting area across from the nurses' station. I will go now and get him. I don't want you to get all excited like I did."

"Before you go," asked her mother, "can you help me sit up and get my purse and help me fix myself up a little? I think I must look terrible."

"You look fine mother. But if you want I'll help you look more beautiful." Jan helped her mother comb out her hair and put on some make up. After she was done she went out and got Tom. When Tom walked into the room both he and Debbie were shocked at what they saw.

"Wow," said Debbie. "Jan wasn't exaggerating. You look very much like my husband," she said almost to herself. "god rest his soul." They stood there looking at each other.

"Well," said Jan. "doesn't anyone have anything to say?" "I don't know what to say," said Tom.

"You look as shocked as I am," said Debbie. "Are you alright?" "I am shocked," admitted Tom. "I'm sorry. my name is Tom Corelli. I'm so glad to meet you."

"Nice to meet you too," said Debbie, "but why are you shocked?" Tom then started by telling of his reaction upon seeing the picture of her with him in the magazine.

"You knew all this when you walked in here," said Debbie. "Why are you shocked now?"

"The last time I saw you, was in your movie about ten to fifteen years ago and yet you look just the same as you did then.

"You remember my movies," asked Debbie being moved by his statement. "my last movie was over fifteen years ago. How can you remember that?"

"I probably shouldn't say this but I had a crush on you. Not only because you were beautiful, all movie stars are beautiful, but because I could see how joyfully and upbeat your personality is.

"That was acting," said Debbie being somewhat embarrassed. "No it wasn't," said Tom. "Even when you played a serious part your eyes were still smiling."

"Are you guys going to sit here and relive the past," said Jan. "I have to go to work. Start talking about what we talked about this morning. I would like to see mom's reaction." Tom started by telling her about the reaction they both had when Jan first saw him and called him dad. He then told her about his reaction when Jan told him her last name. He finally told her about his uncle which finally got to the fact that he was sure that her husband was his twin brother. Debbie was stunned and couldn't say a word. Finally it was Jan who spoke up.

"I have to get to work," said Jan. "I hope that you stick around for a while, Uncle Tom." She kissed her mother and as she started to leave Tom grabbed her and hugged her. Finally Debbie spoke.

"What does all this mean?"

"It means that you are my sister-law. And I'm your brother- law. Janet is a sweet and lovable niece. It means that we are family." Debbie stood with her mouth open. "Hi sis," he then kissed her on the cheek. When she didn't respond Tom continued. "I hear from the nurse that the doctor wouldn't operate because you were depressed. I don't understand. You have a great life. You have a very wonderful daughter whom I already love, so what do you have to be depressed about?"

"It is a stupid reaction," stated Debbie. "I was sad that my best friend moved to California. Then an old geezer bought the house next door. He was convinced that all movie stars are evil and impure. He said that I was arrogant like all movie stars. You are all so above us peasants, he yelled at me. on top of that, I lost my job as a science teacher. Then I got this terrible pain and ended up in the hospital. I felt so alone. I have no family besides my daughter."

"Well you are not alone," assured Tom. "You have wonderful real in-laws that will love you. You have a sister-in-law, my sister, and Peter, her husband. You also have a niece, my daughter Catherine, and a nephew Paul my sister's son."

"I didn't know I had all that," said Debbie with a happy smile on her face. The rest of the day Tom entertained her with wild stories that made her laugh most of the time. They got along greatly. At about five the doctor showed up.

"Hi" he said as he entered the room. "How are you today? I see that you have a smile on your face. Let me check you and see if you are ready for surgery."

"Do you want me to leave," asked Tom?

No," said the doctor."I'm only going to check her blood pressure and pulse." After he checked her he smiled. I think you are much better. I think you are ready for surgery. The only opening I have is monday afternoon. I have a meeting in the morning and a luncheon date, so it will probably be late in the afternoon. I'll inform the nurse and she will prepare you for the surgery." With that said he said goodbye and left. Debbie had a frightening look on her face.

"You aren't concerned are you," asked Tom? "You have to have faith."

"I have faith," said Debbie. "I am a Christian. Are you a Christian?"

"I am a born-again Christian," said Tom. "I go to a Baptist Church."

"That's amazing," said Debbie. "We are born-again Christians also. How is it that you are not Catholic like most Italian people?"

"That is a long story," said Tom. Some day when we have a lot of time I will tell you the whole story."

"Well tell me a short version," insisted Debbie.

"OK," said Tom. "But it will be a short story. A relative changed and when I asked him why he asked me to read the Bible. I started to read and study the Bible and found that the Catholic Church was not following the Bible. one of the main points is in Ephesians chapter 2 verses 8 & 9. What it says is that salvation is free not by works of men."

"That is very impressive," said Debbie. "You know your Bible." "I think we have a lot to discuss someday," assured Tom. "That sounds great," said Debbie. "That means that we will be seeing more of you."

"You can count on it," said Tom. He then started to change the subject by telling her a joke that he remembered by the discussions they had earlier. Debbie couldn't stop laughing the rest of the evening.

The next morning Tom and Jan showed up early in the morning. Debbie was having breakfast. Both Tom and Jan walked up to Debbie and kissed her on the cheek.

"You guys want some breakfast," asked Debbie?"

"We ate a fantastic breakfast," said Jan. "mom you can't believe what Uncle Tom can do. He made scrambled eggs that were out of this world. He adds milk to the eggs which cause the eggs to puff up and it also adds to the taste"

"Sounds like you two have a nice uncle and niece relationship worked out," said Debra.

"Mom he is great," said Jan. "He is very nice and affectionate. He always hugs me when he sees me. I don't remember dad ever hugging me. He is so different from dad. There is nothing of his personality that is like dad's personality." "I'm standing right here," said Tom. "Wait until I go down to lunch. Then you can tell the truth about how you feel about this intruder in your lives."

"Most wonderful intruder," said Debbie. "You brought me out of my depression."

"They brought Debbie her lunch early for some reason. Probably because it was Saturday and they wanted to go home early thought Tom. Tom then decided that since Debbie was eating early that he would go get his lunch early. After he left, Jan approached her mother.

"What do you think mother," she asked? "I see how he looks at you. I think he has more than a crush on you."

"He is just very nice to everyone," said Debbie. "Do you see how nice he is with the nurses?"

"Mom I see also how you cheer up when he walks in. You have it bad don't you?"

"It's that obvious," asked Debbie? "You were so right. He is different from your father. I never felt for your father or anyone like I feel for him. Your father was so serious and strict. All he ever thought was how to be the greatest builder in the country. Tom is so jolly and sweet. I can see how affectionately he is. However, I don't have a chance with him. The nurses talk about him as being a great and famous author.

"You know mom, I don't see dad in him anymore. When he comes to get me in the morning I see Uncle Tom. I don't see dad anymore."

"I know," said Debbie. "I see Tom not your dad. Tom is more slender. He is always smiling. I don't remember your dad ever smiling. Tom is cheerful affectionate and I enjoy his kiss on my cheek more than I did all the love making with your dad. Crazy isn't it?" Tom came back to Debbie's room after Jan had left. They went into the story telling routine with several jokes in between. Near the end of the day before Tom was getting ready to leave, Debbie asked Tom to get serious for a while.

"Tom I don't know anything about you. Tell me about yourself." "Well, if you want to get serious," said Tom, "alright, but first I need permission to call you Debbie."

"I'd love that," said Debbie. "Everyone calls me that. Please do." John then started as he did with Jan from his birth in Cleveland. He told her of his early romances and his marriage to Annie. He described his Job and the novels he had written.

"I would love to read one of your books," said Debbie. "I see you as an incurable romantic. So I think I would love your books."

"Why do you think I am an incurable romantic?"

"It's a good thing. I am one too." Before they could continue the nurse came into the room.

"Sorry," said the nurse, "It's after eight and all visitors got to leave.

Tom kissed Debbie on the cheek and left.

The next day was Sunday. Jan took Tom to South Haven Baptist Church as they had planned the day before. After the service they both went to the hospital to be with Debbie. They both greeted her with a kiss on the cheek.

"Mom, I have to go to work. I traded with one of the other girls so that I can be here for your surgery."

After some small talk, Jan left. Tom and Debbie were left alone. "Now Debbie, I told you my life story yesterday. Now it's your turn to tell me your life story."

"There isn't much to tell," said Debbie. "You know most of my story. I graduated from college and started as a science teacher. I gave up teaching when I was offered an acting job. I found that none of the men in Hollywood were my type. I finally met Joseph at a meeting in Chicago. He was renovating the building the meeting was in. By coincident I met him again at a restaurant I happened to go for dinner. We liked each other and stayed and talked for a while. Some months later I met him in LA. He had gotten a job there. We dated for a few months and after I finish my picture he asked me to marry him. He had one condition. Joe wanted me to give up Hollywood and move with him to South Haven and become the teacher I studied for. I agreed and got married. You know the rest."

"Tell me about your relationship with Joe's supposed parents," asked Tom.

"There was none," responded Debbie. "They were very cold with me. They were angry that he didn't stay in Chicago. I think in all the years we were married they visited us three times.

"Well, let's forget them," said Tom. He then told her a humorous story that got her laughing. They talked about what they believed and the discussion turned to their acceptance of Jesus as their savior. Tom told her in detail how he changed his religion from Catholic to Baptist. Debbie was impressed with Tom's intellectual discussion of his believe. They even talked politics. Even there Tom brought up points that make Debbie laugh. Soon it was time for Tom to leave. Following the same routine as the previous days Tom left.

The next morning Tom and Jan went to Debbie's room after breakfast.

"Mom," said Jan after kissing her mother. "Uncle Tom made me his fantastic breakfast again this morning."

"You will have to make me one of your special breakfasts," requested Debbie.

"I promise that as soon as you get out of the hospital, I will cook for you all day."

"I can hardly wait," said Debbie with a loving smile. They sat down and discussed with Jan all that they had talked about the day before. It was about four in the afternoon that the nurse kicked Tom and Jan out of the room.

"I'm sorry," said the nurse. "I have to get her ready for the surgery."

"When will she go into surgery," asked Jan.

"I'm not sure," responded the nurse. There are a few tests that have to be done before surgery could be performed." The time went by so slowly. Each minute seemed like an hour. Finally about six- thirty the nurse came in and told them that Debbie was in the recovery room. Just after she left, the doctor can in.

"Everything went fine. She is in recovery. In about an hour she will be brought into her room. Just before that I will examine her and give her a sedative. She will be asleep until early in the morning." "Doc," asked Tom, "Can one of us stay here with her all-night" "oK, but only one of you. I will make arrangement with the nurse." After the doctor left Tom turned to Jan.

"Jan honey, I think I should be the one to stay. You have to go to work tomorrow and I think she will appreciate it if she saw me first tomorrow morning."

"Shouldn't I be the one to stay," asked Jan unsure of what to do? "I am her daughter."

"You are like her right hand," said Tom. "She knows that you are with her in your heart. Besides, you will probably be here before she wakes up. I know that you will not even stop for breakfast. You need the rest more than I." Jan agreed and planned on coming to the hospital as soon as she woke up.

The next morning about five thirty, Debbie woke up. Due to the night light, she noticed Tom sitting there next to her. He looked like he had dosed off. She went back to sleep and woke up again at about seven. Tom somehow noticed her movement.

"Hi there sweet lady," said Tom affectionately. "How do you feel this morning?"

"I don't really know yet," she responded. "Let me wake up first. Right now I feel fine, with just a slight pain under my right breast." "Well the doctor said that you are fine. He will see you sometime this morning to tell you what to do next." It wasn't long after that that Jan walked in.

"Hi mom," she said. "How are you this morning?" "I fine honey.

What are you doing here this early?"

"Mom I couldn't sleep thinking about you. Although I didn't leave until the doctor said that everything went perfectly." After some small talk the nurse come in with breakfast. It didn't look to appetizing.

"It is a little farina," said the nurse seeing the look on their face. "The doctor said that you have to eat lightly for a little while"

"Well listen," said Tom. "Since you are eating I think I will go down to get a cup of coffee and see what they have. I will be right back. How about you Jan, did you have breakfast this morning?"

"No, I'm oK you go ahead I'll stay here with mom. Since she is oK I thing I will go to work later." After Tom left Debbie asked Jan to sit down near her.

Jan, don't you think it is wonderful that Tom came here this morning? I wonder what time he came this morning."

"Mom, don't you know how much he loves you? He never went home last night. He wouldn't leave your side. He talked me into going home but he wouldn't leave.

"I thought all visitors have to leave at eight in the evening. "He got permission from the doctor," informed Jan. "The doctor set it up for Uncle Tom to stay all night. Even the doctor sees how much he loves you."

"Jan, I don't think you are right. He is just a very kind person. Look how kindly he treats even the nurses"

"He treats the nurses kindly because you have made him happy and upbeat. mom you had better talk to him. You don't want to wait until he goes home. You could lose him for good."

"I'll think about it," said Debbie. A few minutes later Tom walked in followed by the doctor.

"Well," said the doctor."How is my patient doing this morning?" "I don't know," said Debbie with a smile on her face. "I am hoping that you will tell me.

"A good sense of humor," said the doctor. "That's a good sign." Then turning to Jan and Tom he asked them to leave for a few minutes while he examines his patient. After the examination he explained his findings to Debbie.

"You are doing better than I had hoped. I will see you this afternoon and perhaps you can go home. If I release you I want you to stay in bed at least one day and take it easy for a couple of weeks. I will have a nurse come to your home twice a week to change your dressing."

"How long will that be," asked Debbie.

"That all depends on how quickly you heal. It could only be a week or two."

"Thank you doctor," said Debbie as he left. After Jan and Tom came in and asked what he said she kept all the information to herself. She didn't want them to worry if it didn't happen as soon as the doctor had guessed. All she said was, "Everything is fine." At noon Jan left and Debbie and Tom when back to their usual routine of jokes and laughter.

It was about four in the afternoon the next day when the doctor came back in. Tom was asked to leave and the doctor examined Debbie. When he was through he asked Tom to come in the room. "I think she is well enough to go home. Would you like to go home," he asked Debbie.

"Does a bear poop in the woods," asked Debbie?

"Well," said the doctor, "If you clear with the financial people down stairs you can leave this afternoon." After the doctor left Debbie turned to Tom.

"We have to talk. First when are you going to leave and go home?"

"Are you trying to get rid of me now that you are well," kidded Tom.

"I don't know what your plans are," said Debbie ignoring his comment, "but we have to clear up our relationship, besides being in-laws.

"What are you driving at," asked Tom.

"You said that you had a crush on me when you saw my movie, do you have a little of that left?"

"No," said Tom. "I don't have any of that left. It's much more than that. I'm crazy about you. I have fallen deeply in love with you." "Why didn't you say something before this? It has been driving me crazy," said Debbie.

"I didn't want to tell you because I was afraid to lose you," responded Tom. "I was and still am afraid that you will ask me to leave. I couldn't imagine that you would feel the same about me."

"Why would you think that I couldn't feel the same about you," asked Debbie being puzzled by his remark.

"You are a great and famous star. I am nobody."

"Well," said Debbie. "Think what you want, but I am deeply in love with you."

"Maybe it's because I remind you of your husband."

"I didn't know what love was until I met you. You're nothing like my husband. When you walk in the room I see Tom, not Joe. I find it hard to believe that we thought you looked like Joe. This reminds me of a pair of twins I met in high school. When I first saw them I couldn't tell them apart. However once I got to know then I couldn't believe I had trouble telling them apart. Their personalities actually caused me to see them differently."

"I know what you mean," said Tom "I knew two twins where I had the same reaction. What I am hearing is that you really love me. "Now you have it right," said Debbie. "I never even dreamt that I could feel this way for anyone."

"I feel the same way about you. "I have never felt this way even when I had a crush on someone. I love you with all of my heart." Suddenly Debbie got tears in her eyes. "I'm sorry, is it something I said," asked Tom?"

"Yes, you said you loved me." Said Debbie and then started to laugh loudly.

"First you get tears and now you are laughing," said Tom. "Why are you laughing?"

"It just struck me funny that here we are declaring our love for each other and we haven't even kissed."

"We can solve that right now," said Tom. "However I have to notify you that I may pass out from the thrill."

"I'm the one that will pass out," said Debbie as she got up out of her bed. Just as they were about to kiss, the nurse walked in.

"Hi," said the nurse. "I hear that you are going home." "Yes," said Debbie. "I can hardly wait."

Well, "said the nurse, "if your friend here will go get the release, I will help you get dressed while he is gone."

"Give us a minute," asked Tom. I will get you when I leave." After the nurse left Tom grabbed Debbie and pulled her up tight to him. They looked into each other's eyes for a second and then Tom kissed her. He had been kidding Debbie about passing out from the thrill, but the thrill of the kiss sent a chill down his spine and butterflies in his stomach. When their lips parted Tom could see from the look on Debbie's face that she had an unexpected feeling also. Debbie from the excitement sat down on her bed and Tom now unsupported sat on the chair next to the bed. They both looked each other in the eyes and no one spoke. Neither was able to describe in words what they felt. After a few minutes the nurse came in.

"You better not delay," said the nurse. "The offices close at five." Tom then asked Debbie for her insurance card, her credit card and her address.

"I will see if they are willing to mail you the co-pay. When she had given him what he asked for he left. At the first floor office Tom found that there were two other people ahead of him. When he was able to get to the office window he found that they already had all the information and that they would mail her the co-pay bill. They did want to see insurance card to confirm the information. After getting the release form he went back to Debbie's room. She was already dressed and ready to leave. They had to wait for the wheel chair. When it came, they were brought down to the first floor and Debbie was wheeled to the front entrance. Tom went ahead and got the car. At the car he lifted Debbie from the wheel chair and set her in the front seat. Not a word was spoken on the way to Debbie's house. When they got there Debbie turned to Tom.

"Just a minute Tom," she said. "Here is my key. Take me inside, and put me on the sofa just inside. We have to talk." Tom went out first and opened the door then he picked up Debbie and carried her inside and set her on the couch.

"Are you sure this is oK," asked Tom? "The doctor said you should go right to bed."

"I will go as soon as we have a little talk," said Debbie. When I go to bed I want to go to sleep. I am very tired from the traveling."

"What do you want to talk about," asked Tom. "Tom I want to know what is going on with us."

"It means," said Tom, "that we are madly in love with each other. It means that I will not ever leave you. It means that after you get well that we discuss where we are going to get married and were we are going to live after we are married. We also have a couple of day to decide the details."

"That's all I wanted to know," said Debbie. "Now love of my life take me to my bed and let me sleep." When Jan got home Tom explained to her that he and her mother had proclaimed their love for each other.

"That's fantastic," said Jan. "How soon can I call you dad?" "That depends on you and how your mother wants to handle the future, that is, where we are going to get married and where we are going to live."

"How am I involved," asked Jan, "except that I'm thrilled? I love you already."

"I love you too, but I need you to take me to a jewelry store to buy a ring so that I can propose to her. I think as soon as it's safe to leave her alone we will tell her that we are going to the store to buy food for a fantastic series of dinners. I want to surprise her. I don't want to do it until we can leave her alone."

"Just say when," said Jan joyfully. "I can hardly wait."

The next few days went by as they did in the hospital. Tom cooked most of the meals. After Jan left Tom and Debbie got into the same routine, discussing the past and funny stories. The nurse came twice that week and change her dressing. She told them that it looked well and that Debbie could get up and walk around as long as she didn't overdo it. That Friday, telling Debbie that they went to get fresh food, Tom and Jan went to a jeweler that was owned by the father of a high school friend of Jan. Tom bought a one and a half karat diamond ring and a matching wedding ring. The next week the nurse came on Tuesday afternoon.

"Well Debbie," said the nurse, "You are healing very well. I will change your dressing now but I don't think it is necessary for me to come any more than, perhaps, a couple of times. I think after that you can change the dressing yourself."

The next morning Debbie got fully dressed and came into the kitchen for breakfast. When they were through and before Jan went to work, Tom asked Debbie to sit in the living room.

"Debbie honey we have to talk," said Tom. After Debbie sat down Jan and Tom pulled up chairs next to her.

"First I want to tell you that my daughter Catherine is on her way here. She is going back to college in

Chicago. She wants to meet you and she is bringing two books I think you may like. She can only stay one day."

"That is so great," said Debbie. "I'm looking so forward to meeting her."

"Jan also wants to tell you something," said Tom. "However, she wants to hear your answer to my question first."

"What question," asked Debbie showing a puzzled look on her face. At that Tom got up and kneeling down in front of Debbie with a little black box in his hand which he opened as soon as his knee touched the ground. He lifted it so Debbie could see the engagement ring.

"Debbie, love of my life," said Tom with love in his voice. "Will you marry me?" Tears started to run down her face. She tried to speak but her voice came out as a grunt.

"I think she said yes," said Jan being very happy at the occasion. Debbie got up and threw her arms around Tom. Their lips met and stayed together for a few seconds. Jan interrupted.

"OK you two," she said with joy in her voice. "That's enough for now. You have the rest of your lives to neck." As their lips parted Debbie looked into Tom's eyes and spoke, now getting control of her voice.

"Yes" she said. "I will marry you." They kissed again but a short peck.

"I wanted to see this before I left for school. Now I can start to pack."

"I hope you can stay until Catherine gets here," asked Tom. "I want you two to meet. You are going to be sisters don't you know?" Catherine showed up that evening. When Jan heard that Catherine wanted to get a hotel room she objected.

"We are going to be sisters. I want you to sleep with me or at least in the spare room. If I came to ohio would you let me sleep in a hotel room? By the way if you haven't figure this out yet these two are engaged. At that Debbie showed her the ring. Catherine hugged them both.

"Wow," said Catherine, after looking at the ring again. "Dad, will you have enough money left to pay for my collage fees?"

"It is beautiful isn't it," added Debbie.

"I'm so happy," said Catherine. "Can I hug my future mother?" she didn't finish her sentence when Debbie grabbed her and hugged her.

"You will get sick of all the hugs I am going to give you." "Let's leave these two alone," said Jan. "Come with me and let me show you my room." After they left Tom and Debbie sat down and started to talk about the future.

"Here is what I am thinking," said Tom. "I will stay here until the nurse says that you are well enough to be on your own. Then I will go back to ohio to take care of my house and my business. I would like us to live in ohio. If you agree to move to ohio then this is what I would like you to do. First, sell every piece of furniture you don't want. When that is taken care of ship what is your favorite items to ohio. Then you can stay and sell your house. After selling your house you can come up to ohio and we can plan our wedding. You understand that these are my thoughts. If you have other ideas I would like to hear them. of course if you want time to think about it that's oK with me."

"I have not been thinking of anything else, said Debbie." or at least that has been my dream. I am willing to move to ohio. There we will have a large loving family. I know that by just knowing you and meeting your daughter. I have no one here. I think you are right as much as I would like it sooner we can't plan our wedding until our daughters are home from school. We will want them to be in our wedding party. We will have at least another week or two to think about it.

The next morning Jan and Catherine came down together for breakfast. They were laughing and joking around joyfully.

"I see that you girls get along fine together," said Debbie as she cooked breakfast for all.

"Yes" said Jan. "Cathy and I get along like long lost sisters." "So I see you are close enough to call her Cathy," said Tom.

"I like that dad," said Catherine. "mom used to call me that. You stopped when mom past away. I would like you all to call me Cathy."

It was Friday the next week end that Jan and Cathy left for their individual schools. They all said good bye tearfully. It was on Thursday of the next week that the nurse gave Debbie a good health release and told her that that was the last time she would come to see her. It was the next Saturday that Tom decided to go back to ohio. He checked out of his hotel and before heading to ohio he stopped to say good bye to Debbie.

"I don't know how long it will take to sell the house," said Debbie. "It may not happen until the spring. It is difficult to sell a house in winter. As soon as it sells I will come to ohio."

"I will wait for you with open arms," said Tom. After much hugging and kissing Tom left for ohio.

Three weeks had gone by since Tom left South Haven, and Tom was miserable. He missed Debbie terribly. He was considering on going back to be with Debbie. He found that he couldn't write. His mind was always on Debbie. He was about to turn on the

Tv to watch something that would take his mind off of Debbie when the doorbell rang.

"Who could that be," Tom said out loud? He opened the door, and almost fell over. "Debbie," is all he could say when she wrapped her arms around him and placed her lips on his. After a passionate kiss she looked him in the eye.

"Can I come in," she asked? He didn't answer. He just grabbed her by the arm and pulled her into the house.

"What are you doing here," he asked?

"I couldn't live another day without you," she said and kissed him again. He didn't resist or complain. He was thrilled. When their lips parted he asked her again. "What are you doing here? What about your furniture and house. What is going on there?"

"So you want to talk," said Debbie with a smile on her face that told Tom she was teasing him.

"I'm just afraid that in a few days you will be going back home. I don't think I could take that."

"All right I will tell you everything," said Debbie. "However, after that I want to spend the next couple of hours hugging and kissing.

"It's a deal," responded Tom. They sat down on the sofa and Debbie started her story.

"Last week I contacted the real estate agent. She set up a Red Tag sale. I sold most of the furniture. I gave in to whatever they offered. All I had left was the bed and a few chairs no one wanted. I had the house appraised and told the real estate agent, now that you know the appraised value, go out and get whatever you think is reasonable. I told her that I was leaving the area the next day and to give what was left in the house to charity. I asked her that when all is done to send me the money. I gave her your address. So I came here. I got a room at the Hilton hotel and

I have no plans of ever going back to South Haven again. There now, have you any more questions?"

"No," said Tom and they went into the planned activity.

Tom and Debbie dated for the winter months. Debbie tried to give Tom time to write his book. But they saw each other every night. Sometimes she would cook, sometimes they would go out to dinner and sometimes he would cook one of his favorite dishes, such as his Tilapia fish special. The months went by quickly. During that winter, they did all the wedding planning. They set up may tenth as their wedding day, so that their daughters would be home from school. The wedding was so wonderful and joyful and it was unforgettable. The honeymoon was in Niagara Falls. Debbie had never been there. After they settled down, they lived to help their daughters. Life was great for all of them. Cathy, with Tom's help, bought out an eye glass business. She set up her optometry office there and soon was very busy. Jan got a job as a nurse in the montrose Wellness Center. She ran some of the test performed there. They were all very happy. Cathy had met a young doctor who was there to have his eyes examined. They became friends. They dated often. The months started to fly by. It soon was their one year anniversary.

That day was the happiest day for Tom and Debbie. Their love had grown way beyond their expectation. Everyone was happy for them. Tom gave Debbie a diamond studded necklace. Debbie gave Tom a beautiful golden wristwatch. They were happier than they ever expected.

It was about in the middle of July when Debbie asked Tom to sit down next to her.

"Tom," she started. "We need to talk."

"Oh no," said Tom. "I'm always afraid when you say we have to talk. It usually means you have some unexpected plans. What is it now?"

"Tom" she started. "You know that I love you more than anything. I never even dreamed of being this happy. However, I have had a dream that I wanted to fulfill for you. I have had this dream since we got married. I had almost given up since I thought that I might have been too old.

"You are not too old for anything," said Tom in her defense. "Please Tom," she interrupted. "Let me finish. You see I went to the doctor yesterday while you were in your office working on your book. I wasn't feeling too good. I was concerned about fulfilling my dream."

"Honey, are you alright," asked Tom being concerned about her health.

"I found that I can fulfill my dream for you," said Debbie. my dream was to give you a son. Tom, I'm pregnant with a baby boy." The tears of joy and the passion that came out of the two could not be described. There are no words in English or any other language that could describe the love and happiness that was between Tom and Debbie on that day.

The End

ACCIDENTAL ROMANCE

Dan sat at his desk in his house office reviewing the Publisher'sorder form. He had filled one up for his other books but they had changed it since his last book. This form wanted more details. There were two sections that wanted at least one hundred word descriptions. The first was a book summary. The second was a biography of the author. The book summary was easy but the authorbiography got Dan thinking of his life. He had always wanted to be a writer. Even in high school he would write reports that always got good grades. However, when he graduated and prepared for college he began discussing his thoughts with his parents and friends. He realized that an unknown author would have a hard time making a living until his talent was recognized, if ever. He would have a chance if he knew somebody in the business, but he knew of no one.That was the reason he decided to be an English teacher. Then he could write freely and still make a living. Then his thoughts turned to the problems he had along the way. His father died just as he startedcollege. At the end of his second year in college his mother got very ill and he had to drop out of school to take care of her. She was bed ridden and Dan had decided that they couldn't support a full time nurse and he didn't want to send her to a senior citizens care facility.The tuition money he saved and the money his mother had was enough he decided to take care of her until she got well. She never got well. Two years later she passed away. With the insurance she had and the sale of their home, Dan went back to school. He managed to get a master's degree and got the job at Copley High School that he currently has. Dan was now receiving more money from his novels then he did teaching. His third book caught on and the people who read it decided to see what else the author had written and that sold the less popular books. He had considered quitting the teaching job and concentrating on his writing. His thoughts then went back to the form that he had to fill out. Hewondered how much of his life should he write into the form. Whilehe was thinking he got a phone call. He answered it.

"Hello," said a female voice "Is this Danny Bevelo." "Yes," said Dan, "Who is this?"

"This is Nurse Helen. You have been visiting Roy Been haven't you?"

"Yes I have. Is he alright?"

"He is in bad shape. He has been asking for you. His heart is slowly degenerating. The doctor doesn't think he has very long. We have contacted his only relative yesterday, a granddaughter who lives in Detroit. She is on her way."

"OK," said Dan. "I will be right there." During the summer months, Dan usually joins a church group who call themselves the Hospital Watch. The goal is to spend time and encourage hospital patients who are alone with no family or friends to visit them. The patients whom the members of the group generally spend time with are hospitalized elderly men or women; although that is not a firm rule in that once in a while they visit seniors who are sick at home with no one to spend time with them.

Dan set his form aside and got into his car and left for the hospital. It was ten o'clock when he got there and walked up to the nurse.

"How is he doing?"

"Go in and see him," said the nurse. "By the way he has no idea that his time is short, so encourage him. As I mentioned on the phone we contacted his granddaughter who is on her way here from michigan to be with him." Dan walked into Roy's room.

Good morning Roy" said Dan being as joyful as he could be. "How are you?"

"I'm fine," said Roy. "I feel a little tired."

"Well that is to be expected at your age." said Dan. "You have to have faith. Trust in god and he will take care of you." Dan had been visiting Roy for almost two weeks. During that time he had gently described his love of god and how he believed in Jesus. His goal was to get him to except Jesus as his savior before he was called home to be with the Lord. He felt pretty positive that he had succeeded. Dan spent time with Roy till lunch time when his granddaughter arrived. Before she went in, Dan explained to her that Roy was not aware of the seriousness of his illness. He asked that she should encourage him and to not start to crying in his presence. After she went in to be with her grandfather, Dan left them and went to lunch.

After lunch, Dan approached Helen the nurse.

"I think that my time with Roy is over," said Dan. Who else do you have that could use a friend?"

"There is no one else that I can think of except the woman that was brought in yesterday afternoon," said Nurse Helen. "She was in an auto accident. She came in unconscious due to a heavy blow to the head she had received in the accident. She awoke this morning for a few minutes but only asked for a daughter and then went back to sleep. maybe you can help getting her name and how we can find her daughter. She should be waking up by now if, due to the bump on her head, she is going to at all."

"Well let me try," said Dan. "What can we lose? I don't have anywhere to go." The nurse took Dan to a room two rooms past Roy's room. As they entered the room they heard a low moaning from the woman in the bed. When Dan went further into the room he suddenly stopped.

"What's the matter," asked the nurse seeing his sudden reaction. "Dear Lord," was all that Dan could say.

"Do you know her," asked the nurse.

"Yes," responded Dan. "I think her name is Lilly, no; it starts with an L, Lorna, no, Loretta. Yes her name is Loretta Lane. She was an actress in a couple of Tv movies. Wow, she is as beautiful as she was twenty years ago. She is known as Lorrie.

"Is that her stage name," asked the nurse? "If it is her real name we could use it to find her daughter."

"I don't think so," said Dan. "Besides I think she was married since her movie days. Her daughter would have her married name." Lorrie moaned again and opened her eyes.

"Please call my daughter," said Lorrie "What is her phone number," asked Dan?

"I don't remember it," said Lorrie. "It is in my purse and in my cell phone."

"She has nothing with her except bloody clothes," stated the nurse.

"Who are you," asked Debbie in a very low voice? "Can you find my daughter?" Then realizing she had no idea where she was and that she could hardly move she looked at Dan with sadness in her voice.

"Where am I, and what happened to me?" Dan sat down next to her bed.

"Sweet Lorrie," said Dan with sweetness in his voice. "Just relax and let me take care of you. First, you were in an auto accident and are in a hospital. And secondly, we are trying to find your daughter. Let me start with this question. Shouldn't we call your husband?

"No" said Lorrie, "my husband died four years ago"

"Well then, let's start from the beginning," said Dan. "Where are you from?"

"I live in a suburb of Indianapolis. I was on my way to pick up my daughter at collage."

"Let's start from Indianapolis. What road did you take from there?

Tell me what you remember taking."

"I took route 70 to Columbus. Then I followed 71 to 76. From there I was going to take 77 to Cleveland but I got off at route 18 to get gasoline. my gas tank was low."

"Do you remember getting off 76?"

"Yes I was just getting into a town called lawn something." "Was it called Fairlawn?" asked Dan?

"Yes that is it," agreed Lorrie."

"When you got off do you remember getting to the city of Akron," asked Dan?"

"No," said Lorrie deep in thought. "The last thing I remember is coming to a great shopping area. "What kind of car did you have? give me year and color."

"It was a 2016 off white Lexis," answered Lorrie. "What is your daughter's full name?"

"It is Amelia Benten, which is my married name."

"I think I have all the information I need," said Dan. "I'm going to find your car and see if I can get your purse and anything else I can find. Then I'm going to find and get your daughter"

"Before you go," said Lorrie, "Who are you and how do you know me?"

"My name is Dan Bevelo. "I remember you from your movies. I remember you because I had a crush on you."

"You liked my looks," asked Lorrie being sur-prised by his answer. "You were beautiful and still are. However, it wasn't just your looks that attracted me. All movie stars are beautiful. But there was something different about you. Even when you were serious your eyes always smiled. Your sweet personality showed up in your face. I could see that you are a very loving and affectionate person. You have a very gentle heart."

"You know this just by watching my movie?

"I can see it even now," responded Dan. "Look at you. I know from your injuries you must be in a lot of pain yet you are very upbeat and trusting."

"Wow," said Lorrie sweetly, "I think I have been complemented. go, go get my daughter." Dan smiled and left. Dan drove directly to the Fairlawn Police Station. Fortunately his friend Ronald was still there.

"Hi, Sergeant Ronald," said Dan as soon as he saw him. "How are you today?"

"Hello Danny. Why are you calling me Sergeant? You must want something. So what are you doing here?"

"Yes I do Ron. There was an accident here in Fairlawn yesterday. It was an off white 2016 Lexis."

"Yes," said Ron. "It was pretty bad. The lady that was in it was lucky to be alive. A few inches closer to the door and she wouldn't have made it."

"Do you know where the car is," asked Dan?

"Yes we had it towed to a repair shop. By the way, we gave permission to the insurance company of the guy who hit the lady, to check out the car. His family came and picked him up. He was high on drugs. He will be arrested as soon as he gets out of the hospital. What do you have to do with it?"

"I'm a volunteer at Akron general Hospital and I'm looking to help the lady that was it the Lexis."

"Do you know her name," asked Ron? "We have no idea on who to call"

"Her name is Loretta Benten. I'm trying to find her belongings from the car. She has her insurance card, her cell phone, and all the other information that I need to find her daughter. Can you give me a permission document so I can get her belongings?"

"Sure can," said Ron going to his desk and writing out a permit. "Keep us informed on all that is going on."

"Now if you will tell me where to go I'll see what I can find." "Just take Cleveland massillon road north. Just before you get to ghent road you will find the repair shop on your right. By the way, they said that the car is not repairable." Dan left and had no problem finding the repair shop. In fact the car he was looking for was clearly seen from the road. It looked pretty bad. Dan wondered if they could get inside to find Lorrie's purse. He pulled inside the gate and was met by a middle aged man.

"What can I help you with," asked the man.

"My name is Dan and I came to see if I can retrieve some personal items for the owner Loretta Benten." Saying this, he showed him the police permit.

"My name is Bill. Come I'll see if I can help you." They walked over to the car and it was obvious that they would not get in through the driver's side. They walked over to the other side and the door was partly open but it would not open the rest of the way. The accident had bent the car in the middle and everything was damaged.

"Can we somehow force this door open," asked Dan?

"Wait here," said Bill. "Let me see what I can do with a crow bar." He went into his shop and came out with a large crow bar. With a little effort the door was pried open enough for Dan to slide inside. The purse was on the floor on the passenger's side. Dan was able to grab the car keys and opened the trunk. He took out the suitcases and everything that she had in her trunk and put them in his trunk. He then got a grocery bag he happened to have in his trunk and went back to the car. He opened the glove compartment and placed everything that was in there into his grocery bag. He then grabbed the purse and the bag and thanking Bill he headed for his car. Just as he got in he heard the phone ring that was in Lorrie's purse. He answered it.

"Hello," he said.

"Who is this," said a young lady's voice?

"Is this Amy," asked Dan disregarding her question. "Yes," said Amy. "Who is this," she asked again?

"My name is Dan Bevelo. I am a friend of your mother." "What are you doing with her phone," she asked beginning to worry.

"Don't worry about her," said Dan realizing her fear. "She is going to be fine. She was in an automobile accident. She is in the hospital recuperating. She will be fine. I just retrieved her purse from the car so that she could get your phone number. Fortunately you called. my Job is to find you and bring you to her."

"Are you telling me the truth," asked Amy? "Is she really going to be oK? She was supposed to get me yesterday." Dan could tell by her voice that she was crying.

"Well, first let's get you here and then I will explain everything" "I don't have a car and I have no idea where you are."

"I am in Fairlawn. That is where the accident happened. Your mother is in the Akron general Hospital. Do you have a school mate that is coming this way? otherwise I will have to come to get you" Dan noticed a delay and could hear voices in the background.

"There are only three of us left here," said Amy. "Everyone else has already gone home. Betty is the only one going that way. She lives in Canton."

"Could Betty drop you off somewhere, near here on her way home," asked Dan? Dan could hear Amy talking to Betty in the background.

"No," said Amy. "going to the hospital is way out of her way and she doesn't know how to get there anyway."

"Does she know where Summit mall is," asked Dan.

"Yes," said Amy. "She has been there several times. It is on her way home. She said she could drop me off in front of Bravo. She has eaten there many times. Besides that is the only store she could think of."

"That is great," said Dan. "What time are you leaving so I could be there?"

"Is that too far from you," asked Amy?

"No, that restaurant is walking distance from my house," said Dan. "I just want to know if you are leaving an hour or later tonight." "We are leaving in about five minutes. We just have to put my luggage in Betty's car and we will leave. I just caught Betty as she was leaving."

"Great," said Dan. "It shouldn't take you more than forty-five minutes to get here. I'll be there waiting for you. Look for a white Cadillac. What are you guys driving?"

"We are coming in a blue Toyota," said Amy. "See you at Bravo." Dan left his house a half hour later. He found a parking place in front of the restaurant. He brought a Readers Digest magazine to read while he waited. It was about ten minutes later that Amy showed up. They pulled up behind him, recognizing the car. Dan hit the button that opened up his trunk. Amy understood and transferred her luggage from

Betty's trunk to Dan's trunk. meanwhile Dan got out of his car and intruded himself to the girls.

"Thank you so much," Dan said to Betty. "You saved me the trip and the problem of finding where you girls were. Thank you so much."

"You're welcome," said Betty. Then turning to Amy she waved goodbye. "See you in the fall," she said as she pulled away. Amy then got into Dan's car.

"I don't know how to thank you," said Amy. "I had no way to get here."

"It's about five, said Dan. "Do you want to stop and have something to eat? You probably haven't had much to eat today"

"I haven't had anything to eat since noon yesterday," said Amy. "However, I don't want to stop now. I want to go directly to the hospital and see my mother."

"I understand," said Dan as he pulled out of the parking space and headed for the highway.

"You are Dan," asked Amy?

"Yes but everyone calls me Danny"

"Now that we are introduced tell me about my mother, and how you are involved?"

"Well, your mother got off the highway to get gas for her car when another car went through a red light and hit your mother's car just in front of the driver's door. Your mother got a broken arm, a broken leg and some cracked ribs. She also hit her head and was out till this morning. She was her jolly self when she woke up this morning after learning where she was and what happened. The only thing that she asked for was for someone to locate her daughter."

"What I want know is who you are and how are you involved," asked Amy. "And I don't mean just your name."

"First of all I'm an English teacher. During my off time and during the summer, I am an author. Also during the summer and on weekends I volunteer at the hospital. generally I provide company for older patients who have no family to visit them. I got involved with your mother when the hospital staff asked me to help them. Since your mother was brought into the hospital unconscious they didn't know who she was. Not knowing her name they had no way of notifying her family."

"But my mother is not an old patient," said Amy, and she does have a family" said Amy kind of kidding Dan.

"But she had no one to visit her," said Dan kidding back. "Alright, to tell you the whole truth, I was called in to see if I could find out who she was so that they could call her family. But when I walked in I was stunned. I recognized her as Loretta Lane a movie star."

"But she was in only two movies and that was over twenty years ago. She stopped acting when I was born. How can you remember her?"

"I remember her because I had a crush on her," admitted Dan. A few minutes later they arrived at the hospital. Dan pulled up to the front entrance.

"Go in. I'll park the car and meet you there. go to the blue elevator and go up to the third floor. Your mother is in room 312," instructed Dan. Amy got out of the car and walked in the front door. Dan drove around until he found a parking place. He then walked into the hospital. He was surprised to see Amy waiting for him inside.

"What are you doing here," asked Dan. "Why aren't you up on the third floor visiting your mother?"

"I was afraid to go in alone," said Amy. "I don't know what shape she is really in. I need some to support me."

"You don't believe me that she is fine," said Dan. "Alright let's go." A few minutes later they entered Lorrie's hospital room. Amy hanging on to Dan's hand walked up to the bed and looked down on her mother who was laying there with her eyes closed. Amy tightened her grip on Dan's arm. Realizing Amy's problem he called out to Lorrie.

"Lorrie sweet heart," he said. "Look who I have with me." Lorrie opened her eyes and recognized her daughter.

"Amy sweet heart," she yelled out. "I have been so worried about you. I am so glad that Dan found you."

"Mom," said Amy. "I'm the one that was worried when you didn't show up. I didn't know what happened to you. You are all I have in this world. How are you?"

"Now that you are here I'm a lot better," said Lorrie. "I just have a broken arm, a broken leg and a few broken ribs, other than that I'm fine."

"Well at least your sense of humor is fine," said Amy walking over and hugging her mother and kissing her on the cheek.

"I think my job is done," said Dan. "I will leave you two alone." "Please don't leave," asked Lorrie. "We are going to need your help. We don't know anyone around here."

"Alright I'll stick around if you really want me to. But I will leave and be back in about an hour. I want to call my daughter." After Dan left Amy looked at her mother.

"Mom," Amy asked, "do you have a thing for him?" No," answered Lorrie, "what makes you think that?"

"Mom, I haven't seen you so jolly even when you were well. I can also see it in your eyes."

"Is it that obvious," said Lorrie.

"Yes mom. I don't understand. You just met yesterday."

"I was in such pain, but when he walked in the pain went away. I felt butterflies in my stomach and I got a lump in my throat. I have never felt that way for anyone in all of my life."

"I think he likes you to," said Amy. "Why do you say that," asked Lorrie?

"It is pretty obvious how he sticks around you and looks at you, besides he told me that he had a crush on you."

"He doesn't even know me. How can he have a crush on me?" "He remembers you from your movies," said Amy. "That is why he has gone through all this trouble."

About an hour later, as promised, Dan came back into the room. "How are you girls doing," he asked. "You look like you two have caught up on everything. Was there anything that I could do for your ladies before I go home?"

"We have a problem," said Lorrie. "Amy has nowhere to go. She has no car. mine is wrecked."

"I can sleep in the Hospital Lobby until you can get out of here," said Amy being very serious.

"Who is going to sleep in the lobby," said Sara as she walked into the room.

"Sara, honey," said Dan being surprised to see his daughter. "What are you doing here?"

"I came to see if I could get a job here until school starts up again in the fall."

"Sara," said Dan. "I want you to meet Loretta Lane. This young lady besides her is her daughter Amy." Sara went and grabbed Lorrie's free hand with great affection she enclosed it with both her hands.

"I am absolutely thrilled to meet you. Dad has shown me your movies several times. They are fabulous." She then turned to Amy. "I am so glad to meet you. I would like to get to know you better. Now what is this about someone sleeping in the lobby?" Dan explained how

Lorrie and Amy live in Indianapolis. How she was on her way to pick up Amy at Western Reserve U when a fellow on drugs ran into her sending her here. It's a long story but I got Amy here to be with her mother."

"I'm sorry," said Sara, "but what has this to do with sleeping in the lobby?"

"Well since they live in Indianapolis, and know no one here in ohio, Amy has nowhere to go," explained Dan.

"No way is she sleeping in the lobby," said Sara. "Why can't she stay with me? I have twin beds in my room?"

"Let me explain something to all of you," interrupted Lorrie. "Just before you brought Amy to me this afternoon, the doctor came in to explain all that he did. He said that I had a broken arm, a broken leg, two broken ribs and a big bump on my head that worried him for a while. He said the only bad news is that my leg bones were broken is several pieces. The problem is that the one piece was completely separated. He said that they lined up the bones where they are supposed to be and placed a clamp to hold the separated piece. He said that he hopes that the body will heal the bone in place. If it doesn't then we may need to operate. I asked him what the time frame is for everything. He said that it will be three weeks before he would consider me leaving the hospital. It depends on how quickly the ribs heal. Then it will be at least three more weeks before we can remove the casts. If you leave the hospital you can come to my office for most of the work. my office is on the corner of market and Hampshire road in Fairlawn. However if the leg doesn't heal properly then you will have to come back to the hospital. So you see Danny and the rest of you, I'm not going to be here for a couple of day but over two months."

"So what," asked Dan? "Are we going to let you both sleep in the Lobby?"

"You are coming with me," said Sara to Amy. Perhaps we can both get a job here in ohio. It looks like you will spend the summer here. When your mother gets well why go home. You will only have to come here in a couple of weeks or less. You may as well go to school from here."

"You don't mind having me around all summer," asked Amy? "No, I would love the company this summer. What are you studying in college?"

"I am studying nursing but I am leaning toward performing tests and analyzing test results, tests like X-ray, mRI tests and of course Ultra Sound."

"Look you guys," interrupted Dan. "Why don't you Sara take Amy home and get her settled. I took out a large pizza for dinner. Why don't you heat it and eat. Amy I don't think has eaten since yesterday. Just leave me a small piece."

"You don't mind my leaving?" asked Amy of her mother. "No, you go, I'm not going anywhere."

"Here take my car keys," directed Dan of his daughter. "Take Amy's suitcase and other belongings and place them in your car, then bring my keys back to me." Amy bent over and kissed her mother before they left... A few minutes later Sara brought the keys back said goodbye and went back to her car where she had left Amy.

"How am I so lucky," said Lorrie. "What brought you here?" "I didn't come on my free will,"said Dan being very serious."god grabbed me by the ear and dragged me up the elevator, through the hall way and dumped me in this room." After she stopped laughing she answered.

"I believe that. It couldn't have happened any other way." They both laughed. Dan then brought up a joke that he had heard about a similar incident. After some small talk about their past happenings Dan decided to go home. It was getting close to eight and he was getting hungry.

When he got home the girls were out. He ate the piece of pizza they left him, did some writing and went to bed. The next morning he went down to the kitchen and the girls were there enjoying breakfast.

"Good morning Dad," said Sara. "We have some scrambled eggs for you. We got up early and made breakfast."

"Where were you girls last night? I got home and you guys were not here."

"We drove around so that I could show Amy our town. We also stopped at the mall for a cup of coffee."

"I love this town," added Amy. "I would love to live here."

"I'm so glad that you girls get along so well. I'm going to see Lorrie. What are you girls going to do?"

"We are going to look for a summer job," said Sara. I have a good friend at the Akron general Wellness Center in montrose. I called her and Amy has an appointment at 10 for an interview. After that I'm going to City hospital to see if I can get a job there."

"Pass this information to my mom if you are going there," requested Amy.

Dan went to the hospital. He gave Lorrie all the information he had. They spent the day together. Dan enjoyed her company so much that he started to worry about getting a broken heart someday. But he felt he had no choice. He decided to enjoy what he had while he had it. He was sure Lorrie did not feel the same way he did. If she did it was only gratitude.

That evening the girls showed up about six-thirty. After hugging her mother Amy hugged Dan.

"I don't know how to thank you," said Amy. "You have given me a place to stay. It feels like home."

"It is your home as long as you want it to be," said Dan. "It looks like you are Sara's best friend."

"She is more like a sister," said Sara, "Not only that but Amy got the job. They were very impressed with her knowledge and experience. Unfortunately she has the evening shift. She goes in at 4 and comes home at midnight. I got the job at City hospital but my hours are 8 to 4:30.

"How are you guys going to handle that," said Lorrie being worried.

"Don't you worry your pretty little head about that," said Dan. "We will take care of everything."

"Dad," said Sara, "Can I speak to you alone outside in the hall please?"

"Got something that you don't want us to know about," said Lorrie kidding Sara.

"I promise I will tell you everything when the time is right," promised Sara. After they got into hall Sara turned to her father.

"Dad," she started. "I didn't want to put pressure on you in there, but we are going to need help. I talked to Amy about renting or buying a car, but she said that she couldn't afford one. What do we do? Could you bring her to work at 4 and I will pick her up at midnight?"

"That will be hard on you since you have to be at work at eight the next morning," said Dan being concerned for his daughter. "How about your friend Troy, He buys old cars and fixes them Does he have a car we could buy from him?"

"I already call him," said Sara. "He has a small Toyota that needs an engine overhaul. He thinks he will have about $2000 in it. He is willing to sell it to me at cost. You know he does this as a hobby. He gets these cars in the junk yards and fixes them."

"That's not too bad," said Dan after thinking about it. "I think it will be worth it. Tell Troy that you will take it. offer him about $500 more."

"That would be great. I think a lot of Amy. She is a very nice person. She is worth it. You know that she is a born again Christian.

Her mother brought her up very well."

"How soon will the car be ready," asked Dan?"

"He said it will take about three more days. Since today is Tuesday it should be ready by Saturday."

"That will be fine. Let me know for sure when you know his cost and I will write you out a check."

"I guess you will take her to work the rest of this week then," asked Sara.

"Yes," said Dan. "Let's go inside, but let's not tell them about the car yet." When they went back in the hospital room Lorrie was the first to speak.

"Well," she asked. "Did you get everything settled?"

"You have to understand that I didn't want to put my dad under pressure," said Sara. "I wanted it to be his decision."

"And what decision was that," asked Lorrie.

"Dad decided to bring Amy to work every day at four and I will pick her up at midnight."

"You didn't put pressure on your dad yourself did you," kidded Lorrie.

"I am sorry to put you through this," said Amy. "I will repay you somehow, some day."

"Don't worry about it," said Dan."Why don't you girls go home? I will come home in about a half hour and cook that fish I took out of the fridge this morning."

"Wow," said Sara. "You have not tasted anything until you have tasted dad's special fish dinner. It's his private receipt." The girls left and Dan turned to Lorrie.

"I feel like I need more time with you. The girls have taken too much of our time."

"I appreciate the time you have spent with me and how you have cared for my daughter."

You daughter is so easy to like. I am beginning to think of her as my daughter."

I know what you mean. I'm beginning to feel the same way about your daughter. She is so pleasant. You both are fantastic people."

The next few days went by without incidents. Dan and Amy came to see Lorrie in the mornings. They left about two- thirty every day. Dan took Amy to work at four, and then went home and did some writing. At midnight he would pick up Amy at work and bring her home. Because they got to bed late they would not get to the hospital until ten-thirty or eleven. It was on Thursday the following week that Sara brought the car home she got from Troy. Dan wrote out a check to pay for it and then took Amy to the Auto Bureau where she got the title in her name and got an ohio license. She also got her Indiana driver's license transferred to an ohio driver's license.

"All is finished," said Dan. "Now Amy, you are the proud owner of an automobile. I no longer have to drive you to work." Amy was so happy she hugged Dan.

"I don't know how I can ever thank you. What did it cost you including the license you just got me? Somehow I will pay you back." "Don't worry about it," assured Dan. "I get a great enjoyment out of all this. Besides you are a very special person. If you don't believe me ask Sara."

"Are you doing this because you have a thing for my mother," asked Amy with a silly smile on her face. "I see how you look at her and all you are doing for her,"

"Is it that obvious?" said Dan not holding back his feelings. "It has a little to do with it, but honestly I like you and respect you for yourself. You are really special to me. Please don't tell your mother. I don't want to lose her. I don't think she feels the same way about me. If she has any feelings it will certainly be gratitude."

"I don't think so," responded Amy. "Time will tell."

The next day went as the days before. Dan went to see Lorrie in the morning. He left at the usual three as he did when he had to take Amy to work. He didn't want to tell Lorrie of Amy's car yet. He was tired of hearing all the commotions of gratitude. He wanted things to remain the way they were. Things did change however. That night when Amy got home every one was in bed. She was too excited to go to bed. She wanted to talk to someone. However she decided to wait until breakfast before Sara left for work. At breakfast as they all sat down to eat Amy very excitingly started to talk.

"Listen everyone, I have some exciting new to tell you," she said. "my boss at work called me into her office yesterday. I wanted to tell you all but you were all in bed."

"So what is the good news," requested Sara?

"Martha, my boss, said that she was very pleased with my job and how much I knew. She was impressed on how I could read the results of the tests, to make sure they would show what was required by the Doctor."

"So did she give you a raise," asked Dan? "You have only been there a little over a week. That is pretty impressive. However, I'm not really surprised. You deserve it."

"There is more, said Amy with a very happy smile on her face. "She said that she wanted me with her in the first shift. Starting monday, I will work from eight to four-thirty."

"That's great," said Dan. "You can come see your mother after we have dinner together. I will go in the morning and leave in time to cook a nice dinner for us." Soon after a small discussion, mainly between Amy and Sara, planning on what they can do now that they couldn't do before, the girls went to work. Dan went to the hospital and brought Lorrie up to date.

The days went by rapidly after that. Dan would visit Lorrie in the morning leaving about three in the afternoon to go home to cook for the girls. In the evenings Amy and Sara would visit Lorrie for about an hour until they had to leave. Dan went with them a few times but decided he was not needed. most of the time was spent with Amy telling her mother all the things that happened during the day at work. Dan thought that he spent most of the mornings with Lorrie and that he didn't want to be a nuisance. He explained that since the girls were there that he should spend some time writing. It was in the fourth week of Lorrie's hospital stay that the doctor did a full examination and reported back to Lorrie. Dan happened to be there when the doctor came in.

"Well," said the doctor. "I think you are doing better than I expected. I believe you're good enough to leave the hospital. In about two week I would like to see you in my office. If everything is good I may remove the cast on your arm. Your leg is a different story. I will check it also but I want to make sure the bones heal connecting to each other. The exam I made today is encouraging; it looks like the bones are growing together. When I remove the cast about a month from now we will see if the bones are properly healed. Therefore I am releasing you from the hospital. make sure you get the release form from the financial office." With that said he said goodbye and wished her good luck. Lorrie got tears in her eyes.

"What am I going to do now," she asked? "I don't have anywhere to go. I was hoping that the doctor would keep me in the hospital."

"What are you talking about," asked Dan being confused?" "maybe I can get a room in one of the care centers," said Lorrie ignoring Dan's statement. "maybe you or the nurse could find me one." The nurse happened to walk in as Lorrie said that.

You are on your own, honey," said the nurse as she checked the closet for Lorrie's cloths.

"First of all you can't afford a Nursing Home," said Dan. "You are too well for the insurance to pay for it. Secondly, arrangements have already been made for you. Do you really think that your daughter and I didn't anticipate this happening?'

"I'm sorry," said Lorrie. "I'm sure you two have given this more thought then I have. So where am I going?"

"You are going home with me," said Dan with a positive tone. "We have a place all set up for you."

"No, said Lorrie, "I can't let you do that. You have done more for me and Amy then anyone has ever done. I can't impose on you anymore. Thank you for your offer any way."

"It's all set," said Dan sternly. "You don't have any choice. I'm going to the car to get some good clothes that Amy got for you in case this happened. I also will stop and get your release form. Amy already gave you insurance card to the office. All I have to do is pay for the co-pay." Lorrie was so surprised by Dan answer that she couldn't say a word. Dan noticed her shock look and he smiled at her. "I'll be right back," he said with affection in his tone.

"I'm glad you are getting clothes for her," said the nurse who was checking her closet. "She has nothing but dirty blood soaked rags in here. Bring the clothes and I will dress her." Dan brought her clothes and on the way he got the release form. He waited outside until the nurse had fully dressed Lorrie. She came out and informed Dan that an assistant was on the way up with a wheel chair. When the wheel chair came they went down to the main entrance. Dan got the car and pulled up to the entrance.

"Put your good arm around my neck and let me lift you into the front seat," instructed Dan. She did that and Dan gently slid her into the front seat. He then got into the car and started to drive to his house. on the way Lorrie finally spoke.

"Danny," she said with a romantic sound to her voice. "Why are you doing all this?"

"If you have to ask," answered Dan, "You are not as smart as I thought you were." Lorrie kept quiet the rest of the way. When they reach Dan's house he pulled into his garage. "Stay here until I return. I have to get everything ready to bring you in."

"Sure," like I'm going somewhere," said Lorrie trying to be funny. Dan left and opened all the doors up to his bedroom. He also pulled back the sheets on his bed. Then returning to the car, he grabbed Lorrie's arm and gently put it around his neck. He then lifted Lorrie out of the car. He then managed to lift Lorrie so that her body was higher on Dan's chest. That made it easier for him to carry her in the house. He then carried her into the family room up the stairs and into his bedroom. When he got there Lorrie stiffened her legs.

"Wait," she said. "Where are you taking me? This looks like the main bedroom. You can't put me here."

"Don't worry," said Dan really joking with her. "I'm a Born Again Christian. I am going to sleep in another room."

"You know what I mean," said Lorrie smiling at Dan's comment. "I don't feel right taking over your bedroom. Why are you doing this?"

"I suppose you need an answer," said Dan. "First the room is larger and it can handle a walker much easier. Secondly it has a private bathroom off the bedroom next to the window. If you close the bedroom door you will have privacy as long as you want it." Lorrie stopped asking question of Dan the rest of that day.

"Thank you," is all that she said. Dan placed her on the bed and covered her with the bed sheets.

"Remember what the doctor said," reminded Dan. "He said that you should stay in bed the next few days. Don't get up except to go to the bathroom. And when you do need to get up you can let your left foot touch the ground but you can't put any weight on it."

"What do we do next," asked Lorrie?

"Well it is almost three-thirty," said Dan looking at his watch. I'm going down to the kitchen and start to make dinner for us and the girls. They will be home about a quarter to five. Why don't you take an afternoon nap? When dinner is ready I will bring it up to you."

When the girls got home they were thrilled to find out that Lorrie was at home in bed. They immediately ran up to greet her.

Hi mom," said Amy who got there first. After she hugged and kissed her she sat down next to her. "I'm so glad we don't have to go into that dreadful hospital." Sara, who followed Amy, waited for Amy to finish and then bent over and kissed Lorrie as Amy had done.

"It's so nice to see you are better," she said. "Nice to have you home with us."

"Thank you girls," responded Lorrie. "It's good to be here. Has your dad cooked a dinner yet? I'm very hungry."

"Mom," said Amy getting very excited. "Sara's dad has made the best Tilapia fish dinner I have ever tasted. He has made it several times before and it has always been great. I know that you are going to love it." Just as Amy finished Dan came up with the dinner for Lorrie.

"How do you want your dinner," asked Dan. "Do you want to sit up in bed or do you want me to help you go into the Tv room where I can get a folding table for you to eat from."

"Just help me sit up in bed," said Lorrie. "I'll eat here like I ate in the hospital." Dan then helped her sit up and placed a serving tray across her legs.

"Where did you get this tray with legs on it, asked Lorrie. "Did you steal it from the hospital?"

"Do you think we never got sick in this house," said Dan? "Now stop talking and eat your supper before it gets cold." Dan then set a dish with the fish and a small bowl with a salad on the serving tray. Lorrie took a bite and you could tell by the look on her face that she liked it very much.

The next two week went by with the same result. Lorrie was amazed at the great dinners Dan and the girls prepared. A few days after she got there she decided to go into the Tv room to eat. During that two weeks Lorrie often asked to be brought into the Tv room to watch a movie. By the end of the two week she was feeling pretty good as she put it. It was time to go and see the doctor. Dan made an appointment for ten in the morning on the coming monday. on monday Lorrie was very excited hoping that she could get rid of her casts. The doctor ran several tests on her arm and leg. When he was through with the test and his examination of Lorrie and the test results he handed out his hand to her.

"Congratulation," he said. "I can remove your arm cast; however, though the tests show that the leg has healed very well, I would like the keep the cast on for about two more weeks. You can put weight on the leg but treat it gently. So if you will follow me into the other room I will remove your arm cast." After the cast was removed the doctor gave her a sheet which listed the exercises she should do to bring her arm back to normal. "Have a good day." said the doctor. Dan then brought Lorrie home. Using a cane and with Dan's help they walked into the family room.

"Dan," she said as she sat down. "We have to talk." "What do you have on your mind," asked Dan?

"I think we have to talk about us," said Lorrie. "In about two weeks I will be able and will have to go home." Before Dan could answer the phone rang.

"I have to get this," said Dan. After answering the phone he turned to Lorrie. "Lorrie I have to go to the school where I teach. They are calling a special meeting. I can't miss this. my job may depend on it." With that said, Dan left.

It was about an hour and a half later that Dan returned. After he found Lorrie he asked her to sit down in the family room.

"Now," started Dan, "I think you were talking about going home. Well let me tell you that I will not let you go home alone. As for Amy, it would be silly for her to leave her job and go home just weeks before school starts."

"But you have a teaching job to go to. I can't let you give up your job," said Lorrie.

"Well there are two things I have not told you," said Dan. "First the school meeting was to inform us that since the tax bill didn't pass that some changes have to be made. First they are canceling all the sports activities. They are also letting some teachers go. I volunteered to put off my job until hopefully the tax bill will pass in the fall. The second thing I forgot to tell you is that the insurance has paid for a new car for you. We can pick it up any time. Does that answer all your questions?"

"No I have one more thing to ask you," said Lorrie sounding very nerves. "I have very strong feeling for you," she said finally.

"I like you to," said Dan, wondering what she was getting to. He never expected that she would fall in love with him.

"I guess I have to come right out and say it," said Lorrie in desperation. "I am madly in love with you."

"Lorrie that is nice of you to say that," said Dan being surprised at her statement. "of course you are extremely gratified. Don't you think that ninety percent of your feeling is gratitude?"

"Is this a very gentle way of telling me that you don't feel the same way about me," asked Lorrie.

"Not at all," said Dan. "I've had a crush on you since I saw your movie. After I saw you in the hospital and got to know you a little, my feeling was quadrupled. No, I just don't think what you feel is love but gratitude."

"First, let's get something straight," requested Lorrie. "Then we'll discuss the other. What I am interested in right now is how you really feel about me. If I understand what you are saying is that you are in love with me. Is that correct?"

"All right if it will make you feel better I will tell you the truth. I am crazy about you. I have never loved anyone like I love you. I have never felt this way for any one before. So there I've said it, now what?" Dan was surprised to see tears in Lorrie's eyes. "Lorrie, what is wrong? Is it something I said?"

"Yes, you said you love me," said Lorrie. "It was the most wonderful words I have ever heard."

"You are a wonderful movie star. You are beautiful, intelligent, loving, sweet, and affectionate. Why would you like a nobody like me?"

"So you want proof is that it," ask Amy. "Alright here it is. When you brought Amy to me and I was fully awake Amy noticed a change in me. She asked if I had a thing for you. I denied it but she insisted. So I told her that I didn't understand it myself but the minute you walked in the room I go butterflies in my stomach and a lump in my throat. If that isn't love at first sight, what was it? And I didn't even believe in love at first sight. Besides I am the one who can't believe you love me. I'm the nobody. I only made two pictures and was never asked again. You are a high school teacher, a famous author. I was worried that you couldn't love me."

"Are you finished now," asked Dan. "If you are, then what we are saying is that we are crazy in love with each other."

"Yes," said Lorrie with tears in her eyes again. Dan lifted her up from her chair.

"We have one more proof to check out," he said. Dan then pulled her so that their lips were just inches from each other. "If we tend to pass out we will hold each other up. This also will be proof of our love." Dan was kidding when he said that, however as their lips touched the chill that ran down their spines got their head spinning. They actually held each other from falling. After a long session they finally came up for air.

"Wow," was all that Lorrie could say. With affection they looked at each other in the eyes. "Where do we go from here?"

"Your right," said Dan as a thought came into his mind. "You wait right here I will be right back." With that said, Dan left before Lorrie could ask him where he was going. About an hour later he returned.

"Where have you been in such a hurry," asked Lorrie?

"I had something I wanted to do before the girls got home." Dan then went up to Lorrie who was now sitting on the living room couch. Dan then pulled out a small box from his pocket and going down on his knee he opened it and showed it to Lorrie. "Lorrie," he said, "I love you with all my heart. Will you marry me?" Lorrie slid down from the couch landing on her knee next to Dan.

"Yes," said Lorrie. "I will marry you and love you with all my heart, my mind, and my whole body." Dan then put the ring on her finger.They then kissed with passion they had never felt before. After they came up for air they hugged each other. After they separated Lorrie took a closer look at the ring. "It is so beautiful. It looks like it is too expensive."

"You are worth a lot more to me, Lorrie. Don't you know how much I really love you?"

"I'm beginning to see it every minute that I am with you," said Lorrie. "I shouldn't ask this since the last time I asked you, you disappeared. However, where do we go from here?"

"I would like us to get married before the girls go off to school," said Dan.

"Wow," said Lorrie, "that is a little over a month away."

"Is that too long a wait?" said Dan kidding her. You want it sooner?"

"I would have loved it yesterday," said Lorrie. "Can it be done that soon?" Just then Amy came home with Sara following a few minutes later. Dan and Lorrie waited until both girls were there.

"Girls," said Lorrie. "We have something important to tell you." "What have you guys gotten into now," asked Sara? "We can't leave you guys alone for a minute," said Sara trying to be funny. "We got into real big trouble," said Lorrie sticking out her hand showing the girls her engagement ring.

"Halleluiah," said Amy. "It is fantastic. I'm so happy. It's about time.

Can I call you dad?" She said turning to Dan.

"It would please me to no end," said Dan. "How about you Sara, what do you think of all this?"

"I'm so thrilled I don't know what say," responded Sara. "It will give me a mother and a sister. That will make us a wonderful loving family."

"Your father wants us to get married before you girls go back to school," said Lorrie. "What do you girls think?"

I think it is great," said Sara. "Amy and I will help you plan and carry out all that is needed to get it done."

"You guys realize that there will not be enough time to send out invitations," said Lorrie.

"That's fine," said Sara. "We will just have to do all the invitations by phone. I could call all my relative and friends." Dan who had walked out of the room walked back in.

"I see that you girls are all for this wedding," said Dan. "I just called the pastor of our church. He has an opening on August 26. That is about a week before you girls have to go back to school."

"We will make it work," said Amy. "I can call the only friends we have in Indianapolis."

"I will call Uncle Alfonzo and his family, Uncle Joe and his family and all their married children," said Sara. "I can take care of all our family."

"I will call my friends like Nick and Jim," said Dan.

"What are we going to do for a honeymoon," asked Lorrie? "I have to get back to my home and take care of everything."

"We can have a honeymoon on the way to your home. We can spend three or four days in Columbus. In Columbus we can go to the zoo, the museum. There are lots of thing we can visit. After all it is the capital of ohio. We can then spend a few days in Springfield and Richmond, and other cities on the way to Indianapolis. We can then take care of your possessions and we go on a life time honeymoon. Is that oK with you?"

"Yes," said Lorrie. "All I want of the furniture is the living room and the main bedroom. I just bought the bed room last year. I think you will love it. It has a very large man's piece. It has a large section in the middle for hanging suits and dress clothes. At the right and left it has section with shelf for shirts and anything you want to store. It has four doors one for each of these sections. It is a beautiful piece of furniture. outside of that we only have to pack my and Amy's clothes."

"That sounds great," said Dan. "So then let's get working. I need the number of guests before I can pick a venue. So get that as soon as you can."

Sara had a friend that owned a flower shop so she could take care of the flowers. Dan got the name of an orchestra from his niece who had them for her wedding. Everything was in motion. Amy and Sara took care of calling the guests. The number of guests turned out to be thirty-five. The next week after Sara made the telephone calls Dan's uncles and aunts visit him to meet the bride to be. They loved her. Everything went better than they expected. That Saturday the wedding went by beautifully. Dan and Lorrie were in a daze through it all. That night the newlyweds spent the night at the Hilton Hotel. The next morning they got up late. In the afternoon they had lunch with Sara and Amy. They were also tired from the festivities the night before.

"Listen girls," said Dan. "We are going to leave right after we finish lunch. When you girls leave for your schools please make sure all the doors are securely locked. Let's make plans for Thanksgiving.

We will have a Thanksgiving family reunion. I'm sure you girls will have the holidays off. We will do the same thing on Christmas."

Sounds great, dad," said Amy, with a smile on her face. "I love calling you dad."

"I love hearing it," said Dan. "Well girls are we clear on everything?"

"No," said Sara. "We miss you guys already. I would like to have spent more time with you all as a family."

"Next summer you guys are going to get sick having us around," added Lorrie.

After packing their suitcases in the car, Dan and Lorrie left. The girls had tears in their eyes as they watched the car leave. Dan and Lorrie got to Columbus that afternoon. They got a hotel room and planned on seeing Columbus the next couple of days. They did go to the museum the next day but that was all they saw. They were too busy satisfying the butterflies in their bellies. The same thing happened in Springfield. They weren't really interested in seeing the sights. As they left Springfield they realized that the seed they planted in their heart was the seed of true love that will bloom into a life time romance.

The End

A TICKET TO ROMANCE

Ben looked over the memo he received from the Benson Decorating Co. It was a very enticing offer. They offered him a job as an interior decorator. However he felt he couldn't leave his father's business. Ben had graduated with a degree in Architecture. His entrance exam showed that he was above average in mathematics and design. So they recommended architecture as his major. He liked being an architect. Ben's father owned the Bartelli Construction Company. His father had obtained many building and house design jobs for him. When he didn't work as an architect he was a carpenter for his father. He liked the arrangement and wanted to stay as his father's helper. Some day he would take over the business. He really had nothing else to do. His life had become a very lonely life since his wife passed away. Now his only daughter, Annie, was away to college most of the year. She was home in the summers but that was the time of the year when Ben and his father were the busiest, sometimes working over eight hours a day. most of the summers Annie managed to find a nice job in the area. Working with his father was the only distraction Ben had that kept him from being lonely. While Ben was contemplating the information his daughter came in.

"Hi dad," she said as she walked into his office. "What are you doing?"

"I'm just looking over a possible work order," said Ben. "I'm sorry. I didn't know what time it was. I didn't prepare any dinner."

"That's alright," said Annie, "that's what I'm here for. I can show you what a good cook I am."

"I already know how good a cook you are. Remember our agreement. Whoever gets home first does the cooking."

"Saw the sausage in the refrigerator. I have a real desire to cook a special meal. It's OK this time." She did do a great job, and Ben was sure to tell her. While they were eating Annie decided to make a special request of her father.

"Dad," she said, "why don't we go on vacation anymore? I would like to go out into the country and relax for a while. We haven't gone anywhere since mom passed away. I really believe she would want us to move on. Dad, you are still pretty young."

"I thought we were talking about a vacation," said Ben. "How did we get into the subject of my being young?"

"I think we should go to some kind of summer resort for a week or so," said Annie ignoring her father's statement. "We both need some quality time together."

"I will think about it," said Ben and left the room.

The next couple of days went by quickly. Ben showed his father the job offer he got. He also told him that he planned on rejecting it. "You know that is a great offer, but it gives me an idea. We haven't rewritten our business description for a long time. Let's rewrite it. Currently it is, (Bartelli Construction Corporation. We design & build houses and large buildings.)

"What do you want to change that to," asked Ben not understanding what his father was trying to do?

"I would like to change it to,(Bartelli Construction Corporation. We design & build houses and buildings. We also do upgrades and design of interiors of homes and buildings.) That should bring that work to us."

Sounds great dad," said Ben. "That could bring me more work than I could handle."

"Then we can hire some helpers for you," added his dad.

Being satisfied, Ben went home. His daughter was already home. "Hi dad," she said. "How was your day? Here, I got the mail. It is mostly junk mail. You got one from the children's charity. I thought you already gave to them."

"I did," said Ben "I even gave twice. It's probably a thank you note." With that he opened the letter. "Wow," he let out suddenly.

"What happened," asked Annie?

"This charity had a special deal going on," said Ben. "It set up that if you donate you will automatically be entered in the charity raffle. The first gift is a car and there are two other smaller gifts. It looks like I won one of the smaller gifts. Well Annie, you wanted a vacation and it looks like you are going to get one."

"What did you win," asked Annie?"

"I won two tickets to a two week vacation at a place called Bella valley Resort. The pamphlet that came with the tickets says that it is located in central ohio near a city called Burr oaks. The resort is located just north of Burr oaks State Park and at the north tip of Burr oaks lake. It says that what activities you don't get with them you can get at the state Park. What do you think Annie?"

"When do we leave," said Annie excitingly?

"Well,"said Ben."I will have to call them and make a reservation. When can you be available?"

"I can take a two week vacation any time I want," said Annie. "That was understood when I was hired. So set up the date and I will be ready."

Ben called the next day. He was given a reservation starting Sunday August 13, two week from the coming Sunday. Annie was pleased and excited. School didn't start till the first week of September. She even considered just resigning.

The days went by as if every day seemed like a month. Finally the day to leave came and both were ready as could be. They went to church Sunday morning and left after having a brief lunch. They got to Belle valley Resort about four thirty. When they got there they approached the front desk and asked for their rooms. Ben showed the person in charge the two tickets he had received.

"What is your name?" asked the lady at the front desk. "We are Ben and Ann Bartelli," answered Ben.

"Yes," said the lady after look at her computer. "We have a nice room reserved for you and your wife. It has a lounging room, a large bedroom and of course a bathroom."

Wait," said Ben. "We need two rooms. I have two tickets. This is not my wife, it is my daughter. We need two rooms. one night we could handle, but we will be here two weeks"

"I'm sorry," said the lady. "We only have one room reserved for you. The two tickets are for a man and his wife."

"That is not acceptable," said Ben. The lady seeing his irritation grabbed her phone.

"I'm sorry I can't do anything about that," said the lady. "I have to call my superior." She dialed a number and talked on the phone with her back to Ben and

Annie so they couldn't hear what was being said. After a few minutes, she turned to Ben.

"My boss said that I can give you two smaller rooms. We have two rooms next to each other on the third floor, but they are small rooms with a single bed and a bathroom. That is all we have available at this time." Ben turned to Annie to see what she thought.

"That is acceptable with me, dad. We are not going to spend much time in our room."

"OK," said Ben. After signing in they got their individual keys and went into their rooms. About six they got together as planned and went into the dining room for dinner. After dinner they decided to walk around outside to see what was available to experience.

"I think the brochure said that they had a tennis court," said Annie. "I am looking so forward to playing tennis."

"Well you will have to find someone to play with," said Ben. "That is not one of my strong suits."

"Come on dad," said Annie. "You will not be graded on your performance."

"We will see," said Ben changing to subject. As they walked east they came to the animal pen. Several kids were inside playing with the goats, small deer and rabbits. Passed that was the barn. They looked up at the small mountain that was east of the barn. They both enjoyed the wonderful view.

"I would like to go up to the top of that mountain," explained Ben. "The scenery from there would be amazing."

"Dad, I don't think that will be possible."

"I think you are wrong," said Ben. "If you look closely there is a trail that leads around the mountain."

"I see it, but dad how are you going to go up there. It is a long way off. You will need some sort of vehicle."

"I'll ask the front desk if there is a way to get up there," said Ben. They walked farther into the woods following the stream that led to the lake. At the lake they noticed that there were boats by the pier. They walked around enjoyed the open air and the quiet scenery that they didn't notice the passing of time. Ben looked at his watch wondering what time it was.

"Wow," said Ben. "No wonder I feel so tired. It's past nine o'clock. We must be at least two miles from the lodge. Let's go back. I'm so tired. It's been a long day. I would like to be in bed by ten"

"That is amazing," said Annie. "It's so nice out. It's so bright out it's almost like early afternoon." Ben and Annie then turned back to return to the lodge.

The next morning Ben got up, took a shower, and went down to the cafeteria for breakfast. It was about nine o'clock. He was surprised to see that it was full. He also noticed that at the other end of the room there was another doorway. It was probably an outside entrance. He noticed that a few people were sitting on a bench or standing waiting to get a table. Ben was about to turn around and go back to his room when he was distracted by a beautiful woman sitting at a table in front of him. As he was standing there a waitress walked up to the beautiful lady. Ben interrupted.

"Miss," said Ben to the waitress. "How long is the wait for a table?" Before she could answer the beautiful lady turned and answered.

"Here take this table," she said, looking very nervous. "I am going to look for my daughter."

"No, said Ben. "I could never do that. I couldn't live with myself. No, you go ahead and order. I can wait."

"Nonsense," said the lady. Her voice thrilled Ben and gave him butterflies in his stomach. "Well if you won't take the table how about joining me?"

"You won't mind sitting with a stranger?" asked Ben wishing he hadn't said that. But he wasn't thinking very straight.

"Come and sit with me," said the lady. "my name is Janet Levinsen. my friends call me Jan or Janie. I don't like to eat alone anyway." Ben sat down across from her and fought to get control.

"My name is Benito Bartelli. Everyone calls me Ben or Benny. I'm so glad to meet you."

"Are you here on vacation," asked Jan?"

"Yes," said Ben. "It is just me and my daughter. We wanted to spend some time together. How about you? Don't you eat with your daughter?"

"My daughter is a free spirit. She is probably at the tennis courts.

She gets up earlier than I do."

"How about your husband, doesn't he come with you here?" "No," said Jan. "my husband passed away about three years ago.

It's just me and my daughter."

"I'm so sorry to hear that," said Ben. "I know how that feels. I lost my wife about three years ago. I'm here trying to spend some time with my daughter. I have been so busy in the summer, and when I have time in the winter Annie goes to college. So we don't get to see much of each other."

"What keeps you so busy in the summer and not in the winter," asked Jan?

"I'm an architect. Little work is done outside in the winter. most of my work in winter is generally inside work. I have more time in the winter. The construction work in the summer usually requires a lot of over time."

"Do you also do construction work besides being an architect?" "my father runs the Bartelli construction company. I help him build the houses or buildings I design."

"What made you become an architect," asked Jan?

"I really wanted to be an Electronic Engineer," said Ben. "I was in wonderment of how they could send a picture through the air."

"What made you change your mind," asked Jan? Before Ben could answer the waitress brought them there food and they started to eat.

"When I went to college they gave me an entrance exam," explained Ben. "They said that I was very good at math and had an artistic ability. I always liked to paint pictures as a hobby. They said that my abilities are better filled by being an architect"

"Sounds like you made an intelligent choice," said Jan. "I see that you like what you are doing."

"How about you," asked Ben? "What is your field of endeavor?" "I'm a history teacher at Copley High School," said Jan. "I love teaching. I get all summer off."

"Copley High school is about ten minutes from our home. We are neighbors. Anyway, do you come here all summer," asked Ben?

"No, I usually get a job in a department store," said Jan. "Does your daughter follow in your footsteps," asked Ben?

"Not exactly," answered Jan. "Diane is studying to be a science teacher. How about your daughter, is she following in your footsteps?" "No," said Ben, "my daughter Annie is studying to be an optometrist. By the way how come it is so crowded in here? I can't believe that there are this many people registered in this resort." "You have not been here before have you," asked Jan?

"No I haven't," responded Ben.

"Well, the resort wasn't making enough business to keep it open," explained Jan, "so last year they extended the restaurant and made a door in the front of the building. When you came down the road to the door to register, did you notice that there was a driveway that led into the front of the building? That driveway leads to the parking lot for the restaurant. The restaurant is opened to the general public. The lodge you are staying is also open to the public as a hotel. "Thank you for the information," said Ben. "I had no idea." A few minutes later after they finished eating Jan got up.

"I'm sorry, but I have to leave to find my daughter," said Jan. "Like you, I would like to spend some time with my daughter. It was so nice to meet you. I hope to see you later."

"It was nice to meet you too," said Ben. "Thank you for sharing the table and the information." About a minute after Jan left Annie walked into the restaurant.

"Good morning Dad," said Annie as she sat with her dad. "I see you have already had your breakfast."

"Yes," said Ben. "I got up early and had breakfast with the nicest lady who was willing to share her table with me. The place was so crowded that there was no place for me to sit."

"Sounds like you have already made a friend here," said Annie. "Is she here on vacation?"

"Yes," answered Ben. "She is here with her daughter. Just like us she wants to spend time with her daughter. She is a history teacher at Copley High School. Her daughter goes to college and is studying to be a science teacher."

"Maybe I'll meet them later," said Annie not seeming interested. "Have a cup of coffee while I eat and tell me what our plans are for today?"

"I don't know," said Ben, "let's see what is available. I think before we leave I would like to circle the lake in a nice boat. I also think they have swimming down at the lake."

"I talked to the front desk before I came here," said Annie, "I asked them if they had a swimming pool and tennis courts. She said that both are behind the building. Let's start there." After Annie had a small breakfast they walked down the hallway to the rear of the building. out the back door they saw the swimming pool. There were a couple of woman getting a sun tan and two kids in the pool. "Let's go down the hall to the other end of the building," suggested Annie. "I see a door there. I think the tennis courts must be there." As they went through the back door they saw the tennis courts.

"Wow," said Ben. "There are about six courts."

"Yes and they look like real nice courts," added Annie. As they walked down the side of the building toward the courts, they saw a large bench. Sitting on one end was a nice looking young girl about Annie's age.

"I would like to go around the area and look around."

"Wait just a minute," said Annie. She then walked up to the girl that was sitting there. "Are you waiting for a court?"

"No," said the girl. "I am waiting for a partner"

"Is the waiting for a court a long wait," asked Annie?

"No, in fact there is one open right now. I just don't have anyone to play with," answered the girl.

"You are not waiting for someone special," asked Annie.

"No I'm waiting to see if one of the guys playing is willing to be my partner."

"If you need a partner to play with, will you wait for me while I go to my room and get my racket," said

Annie. "I will be your partner. Don't go with anyone else."

"That will be great," said the girl.

"Listen Annie," said Ben, "you go ahead and play with the young lady. I am going to look around and see what is available for us old people. Later maybe I will go down to the barn to see if there is a stable there." After Annie left to get her racket, Ben waked around the lodge until noon, ate lunch and about two in the afternoon he wondered down to the barn. As he approached it he noticed that there was an opening that looked like a stall. Inside he noticed that there were several stalls. In one of the stalls he noticed some activity. He walked in to ask if horses were available for the guests.

"Pardon me," started Ben getting ready to ask his question. When the person who was saddling a horse turned to answer him, Ben stood surprised.

"Hello Ben," said the woman in the stall. "What are you doing here? Are you interested in going for a ride?"

"Hi Jan," responded Ben. "What are you doing here?"

"I'm saddling a horse to take a ride up to the mountain east of here."

"Where is the person who takes care of the horses," asked Ben? "It's not your job is it?"

"No," answered Jan with a smile. "Jack is probably taking a break or something."

"Is it oK for you to saddle a horse and take it out," asked Ben? "Yes," said Jan. "I have done it before. They don't mind. I can saddle up a horse for you if you want to come along with me."

"I would love to," responded Ben, "as long as I don't get kicked off the property."

"I guaranty it," promised Jan. She then proceeded to saddle another horse for Ben. She then pulled the horses out into the open and they both got on them and proceeded east.

"How much of this land belongs to the lodge," asked Ben?

"About a mile down the road you will see some fence posts," said Jan. "All the land after that, including the mountain, is public property."

"How far are we going," asked Ben?

"I would like to go up on the mountain," said Jan. "I have been there before. It's so nice up there. It is so peaceful and looking down on the land below is fantastic."

"How are we going to go up the mountain," asked Ben? "Can the horses climb up the hills?"

"There is a path that goes around the hills," said Jan. "Don't worry, I will get you up and down." After a few minutes they reached the edge of the mountain. Ben now could see the path that wound around the mountain back and forth to the top. After they got part way up Ben remembered another time that he was on the side of a hill.

"You know, Jan, I've been on something like this before. When I was about twelve old, my father was assigned to a job in Arizona. He worked for goodyear Aerospace at the time. They had a plant just on the outside of Phoenix. I think it was called Litchfield Park. on one weekend my father took us to the grand Canyon. That was the thrill of my life. Anyway they had a special trip on horseback down the side of the cliff that led down to the Colorado River. It must have been over a mile down. It took us several hours to get down there. It was just like this path except we were going down. At the bottom there was a ranch, I think it was called the Phantom Ranch. We stayed there a couple of days. It was the best vacation I ever had. I will never forget it."

"It sounds wonderful," said Jan. "You will be reminded of that trip when we come down."

"Except I hope it will not take as long," said Ben. That thought made Jan laugh. At that moment Ben felt completely relaxed with Jan. He still felt the butterflies when he looked at her but he felt much more comfortable now. It wasn't long before they reached the top of the mountain. They found a hitching post that had been planted there for that purpose, so they hitched their horses and sat on a cement bench that had been built at the edge of the cliff. They sat there for a while enjoyed the view. Being more comfortable Ben started to tell Jan all the adventures he had during his life time. He always managed to make a humorous remark on any subject that was brought up. Ben had Jan laughing often. He loved to hear her laugh. It was so comfortable up there. They didn't want to leave. There was a cool breeze that was very enjoyable against the effect of the hot sun.

"I'm enjoying this very much," said Jan, "but I think we should be starting back. Do you know that we have been on this trip more than four hours?" with that Ben looked at his watch.

"Oh my," said Ben being surprised. "It is over seven o'clock."

"I know," said Jan. "It's been so much fun that we lost track of time. We had better be going back. We don't want to be caught going down in the dark." That caused them both to laugh. They both knew that it wouldn't get dark until after nine.

"Anyway," continued Ben. "The fresh air has made me very hungry."

"Let's go some were else for dinner," suggested Jan. "What do you have in mind," asked Ben?

"There is very nice Italian restaurant in Athens," said Jan. "I haven't been there for a while. I used to love their Sicilian sausage. The dinner is on me."

"Do you like Italian food," asked," Ben? "You are not Italian are you," asked Ben? "Your last name Levinsen is not Italian but it could be you married name."

"I am one half Italian," said Jan. "my stomach is one hundred percent Italian. my mother was Italian. my father was german. It was my grandmother who I was closest to. She taught me how to cook the best Sicilian meals you ever tasted. After grandfather died she moved in with us. She took care of me. By the way, my grandfather was a builder like your father"

"Sounds like you had a very happy childhood," said Ben. "I will go with you wherever you take me under one condition. I pay for the meal."

"It was my Idea so let me treat you," said Jan. "Besides, your meals at the Lodge are included in your contract."

"First my whole stay is free," said Ben. "I won two tickets from a charity I donate to. Secondly, I promised myself that I would never let a woman I date pay for anything. I have kept that all my live. Do you want to break my record?"

"Oh god forbid," said Jan with a big smile. "All right let me at least drive us there. You don't have a rule against that do you," she asked? At that they both laughed. The way to Athens was very pleasant. Ben made humorous comments along the way making Jan laugh often. At the restaurant, Ben let Jan order the dinner. It was a sausage casserole. It was the best Ben had ever tasted. After they ate they sat with a cup of coffee each and spent the evening discussing various simple and humorous experiences in their lives. At about nine thirty they decided they had better head back to the lodge. Back at the lodge Ben turned to her as she was ready to go up to her room.

"I had a very wonderful time," he said with a loving look on his face. "I have enjoyed the time we have spent together to day. I hope we can do it again some time."

"I had a real good time," said Jan. "I'll see you tomorrow. goodnight."

The next morning Ben went to breakfast alone. He was hoping that he would find Jan there again but she was not. Ben wondered around the area, had lunch and finally found Annie at the tennis courts. She and her friend were playing tennis together. It seemed like Annie found a good friend. Ben then decided to contact Jan if he could. He went back to the front office. It seemed like a teen aged girl had taken the front desk job.

"Can you give me the room number for Janet Levinsen," asked Ben? The young lady looked up the computer page then at the little booklet on the desk behind her.

"Sorry," she said. "mrs. Levinsen checked out this morning." Ben was devastated. He didn't know what to do. Perhaps he could go home and look her up. Then he had second thoughts. That would not have been fair for Annie. He then decided to go down to the lake and sit on the beach. He was just leaving the lodge when he ran into Jan.

"Hi Ben," she said "I was just coming to look for you."

"Jan," said Ben being surprised to see her. "I was just looking for you. I was so sad because the girl at the desk said that you had checked out. Have you decided to come back?"

"I'm sorry," said Jan with a smile on her face. "The young girl at the desk didn't know what I did. She was right I checked out of the lodge but I did not check out of the resort."

"I don't understand," said Ben.

"I found that a bungalow became available," explained Jan. "I prefer a bungalow to a room in the lodge."

"Why is that?" asked Ben being confused.

"It is more private," answered Jan. "I like it also because I can cook my own meals. I'm tired of the lodge's menu."

"I'm a good cook myself," said Ben. "Perhaps one evening I could come over and cook one of my specialties."

"What is one of you best specialties," asked Jan? "Do you like fish," asked Ben?

"Fish is my most favorite meals. That's one of the reasons I don't like to eat at the lodge. They don't have good fish dinners."

"Well I have a secret recipe for Tilapia that most people would die for," declared Ben.

"Unfortunately, like you have a rule that you will not let a woman pay for your meal, I have a rule that I will not be alone in bungalow with a man. That is a safety rule."

"Well you can make an exception with me," Suggested Ben. "You are completely safe with me. You see, I am a Born Again Christian. I promised god, myself and my mother that I will never dishonor a woman"

"Is that right?" said Jan with a tone of amazement in her voice. "I didn't think there were many of us left."

"Are you a Born Again Christian?" said Ben being amazed himself. That is the best news I have heard."

"I have to tell you the truth then," said Jan. "I don't really have a rule like that. However, before I confess further, let me ask you a question. You are Italian and are not all Italians Catholic?"

"I am Italian, and I was a Catholic" said Ben. "I did change a few years ago. It is a long story. I don't think you want to hear it."

We don't have anything to do," said Jan. "give me the short version."

"One day about twenty years or more ago, I was surprised when my uncle Joe who lived upstairs from my parents, didn't show up in church one Sunday. I was worried that he was sick. When I called, Uncle Joe told me that he had changed churches. He tried to explain, he finally told me to read the Bible. In fact the next time he saw us he gave me a large Bible. I have it now on a stand in my family room. Anyway I studied it and found so many places that I was not worshiping as the Bible directed. I then, after reviewing the different churches, chose the Baptist church because it centers everything it does on the Bible. Also many churches ignore the Ephesians chapter 2 verses 8 and 9 which tells us that salvation is a free gift of god, not due to works so that no one can brag that they worked their way into heaven."

"You amaze me," said Jan. "I guess now I owe you the truth of my actions. I moved because of the problem I was having, and I told you that I didn't want you into my bungalow because of this problem. You see I was having feelings for you and I didn't want to get into another relationship with a non-Christian or poor Christian. I don't want to get into details but my husband was not loyal to me. I have not trusted in a man since he passed away."

"So what is your feeling now?" asked Ben. "Are you still afraid to get involved in another man?"

"I'm still afraid of getting hurt," said Jan. "For example, what if you don't have feeling for me like I have for you. I don't think I could handle that if we keep seeing each other and then you dropped me." "Well you can stop being afraid,"said Ben now being encouraged.

"I have more than strong feeling for you."

"I think I am falling for you," confessed Jan. "The truth is that when I first saw you at that first breakfast, I got butterflies in my belly and a lump in my throat." Ben started to laugh uncontrollably out loud. "Why are you laughing at me? Am I a big joke to you?"

"No, I'm sorry," said Ben still smiling. "I am laughing because I'm happy. You see I had butterflies in my belly and a lump in my throat like you. Couldn't you tell by the stupid remarks I made. I realized that I was madly in love with you when we went up the mountain."

"Why didn't you say something," asked Jan now smiling a happy smile.

"I was afraid I would lose you. I was enjoying your company so much. I didn't think I was good enough for you. I still don't." Jan then grabbed Ben by the arm and pulled him into the woods where they were alone. "What are you doing?" asked Ben being confused by her actions.

"I was so worried that you didn't love me like I love you. I don't think I am good enough for you."

"Let me tell you why I think we are good enough for both of us." said Ben.

"Shut up and kiss me," said Jan when they were deep in the woods. Ben didn't have to be asked twice. Their kisses got very passionate. Soon their tongues got into the act. Their legs got so week that they were hold-ing each other from falling. After several minutes they came up for air. Ben spoke up first.

"Jan I have never felt this way for anything in this world. I didn't even know I could feel this way for any-one. I am so in love with you that there are no words that can describe it."

"Oh Ben," said Jan passionately. "I know what you mean. I have never felt this way before either."

"Where do we go from here," asked Ben?

"I don't know," said Jan. "At our age we don't have time to play games, if you know what I mean. However, we should let my girl meet you and let your girl meet me. That will give us a little more time to get to know each other."

"I know," said Ben. "I am not perfect. So you have to get to know my faults and decide whether you could live with them."

"Can you live with my faults," said Jan?

"You seem perfect to me." said Ben. "At least you kiss is perfect. That will override everything else."

"I agree so let's talk about getting the girls together with us," said Jan.

"I know where to start," said Ben. "my daughter and I have talked about going on a boat ride. Let's invite them right now. You call your daughter and I will call my daughter."

"That's a great idea," said Jan." "But first let's see if a boat is available. Also, I think we should keep our relationship to ourselves for the time being." With that said they went down to the dock. Fortunately one was available that was big enough for eight people. With that done they both got on their cell phones. When they finished talking they discussed their results.

"My daughter will come in about an hour," said Ben. "She wants to finish the tennis match she is having with her friend. However, she asked if she could bring her girl friend with her. I said yes. I hope that is alright with you."

"Yes that is fine," said Jan. "However, I have bad news. my daughter can't make it. She promised her girlfriend that she was going to meet her family"

"That is oK," said Ben. "I can meet her some other time. At least you can meet my daughter." About an hour later Annie came down to the dock with her girl-friend. They walked down to Ben and Annie was about to introduce her friend when Jan broke in.

"Diana Honey, said Jan. "I thought you said you couldn't make it.

What happened?"

"Mom," said Diana. "What are you doing here? I came to meet Annie's father."

"Isn't god wonderful," said Ben. "Annie's best friend is Diana your daughter. Isn't that wonderful? We can now get to know each other."

"I can't believe what I am seeing," said Jan, being in total amazement. "What a wonderful turn of events."

"Are you two friends," asked Annie?"

"Yes," answered Ben. "We have been spending time together." "Let's stop this small talk and let's go boating," suggested Jan, wanting to end the question-ing for now. They all got into the boat and with Ben at the wheel they enjoyed viewing the lovely houses along the shore line.

"I believe that this lake is about four miles long and about one and a half mile wide at the southern end," said Ben. "I will keep it close to the shore so we can see the beautiful homes built along the lake."

"You are right about the size of the lake," added Jan. "You have been doing your homework. If you travel at about four miles an hour it will take about an hour to get to the north end of the lake. If we go down the other side of the lake for about an hour we will get to a boat dock. Above the dock is a restaurant. It has very good food. It is about three now. We will be get-ting there between five thirty and six. I suggest that we stop there for dinner."

"Wow," said Ben. "Did you have this all planned ahead of time?" "No," responded Jan. "I just have been through this before" "Well it sounds like a great plan to me," said Annie.

"Me too," added Diana.

"So let's do it," said Ben. "We can all eat together which we have not done before."

"Will that break another of your rules," asked Jan laughingly. "What's this about a rule," asked Diana?

"It's an inside Joke, said Ben, "it's too long to explain."

"It's that Ben here has a record of not letting a woman ever pay for a meal."

"That's my dad," said Annie. No more was said on the way to the north side of the lake. They all enjoyed the scenery along the way. on the way down the other side they began seeing a more luxurious set of houses. The conversation from there to the restaurant was about the fantastic building and back yards that they saw. At the restaurant the girls couldn't stop talking about the amazing things they saw. When the main meal was finished they sat there with a cup of coffee having general conversations. Ben got started telling funny things that happen to him on other vacations and he finish the evening telling jokes urged by his daughter who loved her dad's stories. They were having so much fun that they didn't notice the passing of time. By the time they realized the time it was after eight. They decide to return to the lodge by crossing directly across the lake rather than around the shore line.

The next morning, Ben and Annie ate breakfast in the morning and then they went to Jan's bungalow. Jan and Diana were just walking out. Diana got together with Annie. They decided on several things they wanted to do together for the rest of the day until dinner. After the girls left, Ben took the opportunity to hug Jan and kiss her passionately.

"Where are you going," asked Ben.

"I was going to buy something for dinner," said Jan. "It looks like Diana is going out with Annie. I had Diana promise me that she and Annie will be home for supper so that we can all be together. I was coming to invite you. I think the girls are aware of what is going on.

"I know, said Ben. "However, I was planning on getting some Tilapia and giving you and your daughter a taste of my special dinner."

"That will be great," said Jan. "How about we doing that tomorrow night. "I am all set on giving you a taste of my own special dinner. It is a Standing Rib Roast dinner which is cooked with a special sauce coating."

"That's a good idea," said Ben thinking it over. "I will need some special hardware and spices to cook it the way I do. Let's go inside and see what you have. Then we can go to the store and get all the things you need and the things that I need that you don't have." They went inside and Ben took a note of what he needed that was not available in this bungalow kitchen. Ben found that they had only one of the pans that he need, besides some of the spices. So, he had to buy another pan. After a full search of the kitchen they left for the city.

That Evening they had Jan's special standing rib roast. Annie and Ben were surprised at how good it all was.

"After this superb dinner I'm afraid to cook mine," said Ben? "It will never meet you dinner. I won't ask you what the special ingredients were. They were fantastic."

"Don't worry, Dad," said Annie. "This dinner was the best meat dinner I ever had but I think your fish dinner will come up to the same standard."

"Will you guys stop flattering me," said Jan. "You are going to spoil me." They all had desert and after some jolly conversations Ben and Annie left to go back to their rooms.

The next day went the same as the previous day. Annie and Diana went to play tennis and Ben and Jan enjoyed the day together. There were times when their passion got too great, and they had to go outside to cool off. That evening Ben made his special Tilapia dinner. They all couldn't express in words how great it was.

"Mr. Bartelli," said Diana, "I have a confession to make. You see I generally don't like fish. I hate the fish taste. I didn't say anything because you have been so great I didn't want to hurt your feelings. However, I admit that I have never tasted anything, meat or fish that tasted this great. I think I am going to be a fish lover. Are there any other fish that you can cook this way that will taste as great?"

"Yes," responded Ben. "There is catfish and salmon that I have had similar success. It took a little more finesse with salmon. You see I don't like fish taste either."

"You will have to make me some of both someday," requested Diana.

I would love that," said Ben. "one of these days I will surprise you."

"Look Ben," said Jan. "You and I need to have a little talk." "What is the problem," asked Ben?

"Just come with me and I will explain," said Jan. "You girls go do your thing." Jan then grabbed Ben by the hand and pulled him across the way into the wooded area.

"Ben," she started. "I have not been honest with you.

"You have a boyfriend or a fiancé?" asked Ben beginning to worry.

"No, it's nothing like that," said Jan. "I just don't like to tell anyone so that it will not affect their reason for liking me."

"I don't understand," said Ben. "Do you have some kind of record you don't want people to know about?"

"Please don't ask questions,"asked Jan."It's hard enough without other questions. What I want to tell you is that my grandfather was a farmer out here. When farming was not doing so good he decided to build a hotel on his land to add to the income of his farm. As time went by his hotel business grew, and the farm got smaller. What I'm trying to tell you that my father inherited it and now has given it to me lock stock and barrel. What I'm having a hard time telling you is that I own this resort. I own the lodge the bungalows and everything on this land up to the lake."

"Wow," said Ben. "That is why you were able to get a bungalow so easily. But why were you afraid to tell me?"

"I'm afraid that people would want to come close to me because I had money."

"Well you don't have money," said Ben. "Everything you have is tied up in this resort area."

"Why do you say that?" asked Jan being surprised in Ben's statement.

"Because if you had money you wouldn't be teaching and have your daughter working during the summer. Besides, either way, I don't care. I don't need your money.

"Your something else," said Jan. "Every minute I'm with you I fall more and more in love with you. However, I think you are too smart for me."

"Don't ever forget that," said Ben with a big smile on his face. That smile also made Jan laugh. When they went back to the bungalow the girls were watching a movie on Tv. It was a murder mystery. Ben and Jan got interested and watched it with them. After the movie, Jan took out some cookies and made some coffee. They sat there discussing the strange ending to the movie. When it got late, Ben and Annie went to bed at the lodge.

Ben and Jan spent the rest of the week together. Twice they went riding on horseback. They went one more time up to the mountain and once through the woods. They enjoyed each other's company. The girls most of the time would go out on their own. However they would always have dinner together with Ben and Jan. Sometimes they would eat in the city. Ben had the opportunity to cook one of his catfish dinners and one of his salmon dinners. They enjoyed both very much. The rest of the week Jan did most of the cooking. Finally on the Friday before they had to go home, Ben cooked his Italian Spaghetti dinner.

"That was the most delicious dinner I ever had," said Diana. "You will have to cook this again after we all go back to northern ohio.

"I will like to do that," said Ben. "That brings up another question that I have been thinking about. I was wondering if we could stay here another week or so. Then I could cook some of my other special Italian dinners."

"That is a great idea," said Jan. "I wouldn't have any problem with that."

"I would have a problem with that," said Annie. "I promised to be back in two weeks. Besides, I am learning so much on all the eye testing instruments. I don't want to stay here any longer. I want to go home tomorrow as planned."

"Me too," said Diana. "I need to go back to work also."

"I understand," said Jan. "I have another idea. I'm sure you girls know that Ben and I are interested in each other and that is why we want to stay longer. So what if you Diana take my car and go home." You can take Annie with you and drop her off at her house. Ben can take me home in his car when we decide to come home.

"Yes that will work," said Ben. "We will see if I can keep my room at the lodge."

"That will be no problem," said Jan. "They will not kick you out once you're here." With that settled they had desert and spent the rest of the evening watching a romantic movie.

The next morning they all meet at the lodge restaurant for breakfast. Ben and Annie were surprised to see them there.

"What are you guys doing here," asked Ben? "We ran out of milk and eggs," said Diana.

"I was so interested in the dinner that I forgot to buy what I needed for breakfast," said Jan. "Anyway Ben and I will probably be eating breakfast here after you girls leave."

"She is kidding," said Diana. "We came to the lodge to ask you to come to the bungalow to have breakfast with us. This is the last day we will be together. When we got here we saw that you were already eating here at the restaurant. So I guess we will eat here with you."

"That is so sweet," said Ben. "I like the idea that we spent this time together. Do you girls have any plans for this day?"

"I think this morning and early afternoon Diana and I would like to spend the day together," said Annie. It will be our last day together. We however will be back early to spend the evening with you all."

"Sounds great," said Ben. "I would like to spend this day with Jan.

I have a special place I want to go."

"What do you have in mind dad," asked Annie?

"You and Diana will find out tonight," answered Ben. After breakfast was over they remained together for a while drinking coffee. After the girls left, Jan turned to Ben.

"What do you have in mind," she asked.

"I want to confirm our relationship," said Ben. "How do you want to do that," asked Jan?

"Take me to a jewelry store and I will show you," answered Ben. "one of our old friends, the one that Diana went to see the other day, martha, well her father has a jewelry store. I'm sure he will give you a fair price. "Why do you want to buy me a necklace or a bracelet, or perhaps something for Diana?"

"Something like that," said Ben. Nothing was said after that. Jan drove Ben to martha's father's jewelry store. When they got there the owner hugged Jan seeing who it was.

"Jan, how are you?" he said. "I was wondering if you would come down to see me. I saw your daughter the other day. It is so good to see you.

"Ben, I want you to meet mr. Sam marten," said Jan. "He is martha's father. mr. marten, this is a good friend that we met at the resort."

"What can I do for you," asked mr. marten?

"Ben wants to buy me a piece of jewelry so that I will not forget him," said Jan. mr. marten turned to Ben.

"I really like this girl so I want to ask her to marry me, but I can't because I need a ring," said Ben. He was surprised when he looked at Jan's face. She had a shocked look on her face and tears in her eyes. Ben couldn't believe that she didn't really expect it. Did she really believe that all he wanted to buy her was a simple necklace or something like that?

"Do you have anything in mind," asked mr. marten?

"Yes," said Ben. "I would like a ring with a one and a half carat main diamond, with smaller diamond on each side of it."

"I have just the one you want," said mr. marten as he walked into the back room. A few minutes later he came out with a small box. He opened it and showed them the most beautiful ring either Ben or Jan had ever seen. "It is special in another way," continued mr. marten. "The wedding ring can be attached to the engagement ring. You just have to push the wedding ring against the engagement ring and turn it. It then becomes attached to make it look like one ring."

"I love it," said Ben. He then looked at Jan. She couldn't talk but she did shake her head up and down suggesting that she liked it. "How much," asked Ben?

"I can give you both rings at my cost," said mr. marten. "I will do this with respect to Tom Levinsen, Janet's father. He did so much for me. If it wasn't for him I would not have this store." Ben agreed to the price mr. marten gave him. After paying for them Ben kneeled down in front of Jan.

"Jan," started Ben. "I love you more than words can express. I want to spend the rest of my life with you. Jan, love of my life, will you marry me?" Jan was still in a state of shock. However, not wanting to pass up the dream of her life, she knelt next to Ben and forced out the word yes and gave him the most passionate kiss he had ever received. Ben put the ring on her finger and they both went back to Jan's passionate kiss. Suddenly they were alone in the world. When they final can back to reality they heard loud clapping. Several other customers had entered the store and were now clapping at the romantic scenery they were witnessing. on the way back to the resort they were both in a state of shock. They barely remember driving back. When they got back to the bungalow Jan pulled Ben in the living area and they both sat on the couch and went into passionate necking. They broke it off a couple of times when they felt there passion was going too far. After a few minutes to cool off, they went back to their necking. This continued until they hear a noise in the front door. It was the girls coming home to be with them. Ben looked at his watch.

"Dear Lord," said Ben."It is five o'clock. We haven't even started to make dinner."

"Who wants to eat," responded Jan. "I'm sure the girls are hungry," said Ben.

"What is going on," said Diana after they walked into the living room. "I don't smell one of your meals cooking in the kitchen."

"How would you girls like going out and celebrating," asked Jan?

"You want to celebrate getting rid of us," kidded Diana.

"We want to give you a very happy parting party," kidded Ben right back.

"I know," said Annie. "You guys got so busy making love that you forgot to cook."

"You are smarter than I gave you credit for," said Jan. "You are partly right. We were necking all afternoon and did forget to cook. However, that is not why we want to celebrate. We want to celebrate the action which brought you two one step closer to becoming part of one big family." Jan saw the confused expression on the girls faces, so she stuck out her hand so the girls could see the ring. "This is what we want to celebrate," added Jan.

Wow," said Diana, and then looking at Ben she said. "Can I start calling you dad?"

"Only if I can start calling your mother mom," said Annie as she went over to Jan and hugged her. Seeing that, Diana went over and hugged Ben.

"I can't think of anything that pleases me more," said Diana. "I think it is a very good reason to celebrate. I now wish I didn't have to go home."

"Me too," said Annie. "I can't think of anything that has ever make me happier." After some happy discussions of what that meant, they all went to a restaurant in zanesville. They went to a large restaurant where they had never been before. It turned out to have been a wonderful decision. Everything was fantastic. After a jolly time, the evening came to an end. They all went home and with sadness they said goodbye.

"When will we ever be together again," asked Annie?

"We will get together when we get home before you girls go to school," said Ben. With that said they all went to bed.

The next morning Ben got up early. He didn't sleep much all night. His thoughts were on his future new family. He wanted to continue what they had last night. Suddenly it became clear to him what he had to do. He hoped he wasn't too late. He called his daughter's room number. Fortunately Annie answered.

"Honey," said Ben. "What are you doing?"

"I'm starting to pack to get ready to leave. Diana wanted to leave early."

"Go ahead and pack but don't go anywhere until I call you. There may be a change of plans." With that he hung up and headed for the bungalow. When he got there Diana was ready to leave.

"Diana honey," said Ben. "Don't go anywhere yet. There may be a change of plans. Is your mother up yet?"

"Yes we had breakfast together." Ben went to the door and knocked. When Jan answered the door, Ben stepped inside.

"Jan honey," Ben started. "I couldn't sleep last night. I think we should change our plans. I think we should leave with our girls. I was thinking that the girls will have a little over two week before they go back to school. I think we should spend that time with them while we can. We can be a family together every evening. After they go back to school we can only see them on a holiday if then. After they graduate, who knows where they will be located. Hopefully they will be around us but we can't be sure they both will."

"I'm so glad you came up with this, "said Jan. "I was having the same thoughts. I was feeling so sad. We can still be together. It is just a little farther from my house to yours then it is from the lodge to the bungalow. So what? Let me go and pack up so we can leave with the girls. I will drive my car with Diana. I will meet you in front of the lodge. We can follow each other home. You explain this to Diana while I pack." Ben didn't have to explain. Diana hear everything through the partially open door way. As Ben came through the door way Diana hugged him.

"Dad," said Diana. "I hope Annie is as happy about this as I am." Ben left to pack. At the lodge Ben filled Annie in and she was just as happy about the change as Diana was.

On the way out Jan pulled her car behind Ben's car which was parked in front of the lodge. She got out and walked up to the car. Ben and Annie were there waiting for them. Ben opened his window. "Ben," started Jan. "I have been thinking about where to go from here. We don't have any food at home and I don't think you have any either. So I think we should follow each other into the Akron area and then each goes home. We should each go shopping for food. You and Annie then come to my house around six for dinner. Here is my address. We can come to your house for dinner tomorrow. What do you think?"

"Sound great," said Ben. "We will see you at six. Ben waited for Jan to get back into her car and then they left for their homes.

At five thirty that evening Ben and Annie set out for Jan's house. They had stopped at the grocery store that afternoon and Ben purchased what he needed for a salmon dinner the next day. All the houses were beautiful in the montrose area. Jan's house was smaller but just as beautiful. Jan made the standing rib roast that Ben loved. The next night they ate at Ben's house. They alternated until Saturday. It was Jan's turn.

"Saturday is my day off," said Jan. "We have two choices. We either go out for dinner or we order a nice hot pizza."

"Let me order the pizza," said Ben. "I think we have a few things to talk about that are better said here at home."

"I agree," said Jan. "do you girls mind?"

"No," said Annie. "I think we need a more normal day. You guys are going to spoil us with all that good food. We need a more normal dinner. Besides I think we do have many things to talk about. Diana and I have talked about some of the things that I thing we should discuss."

"The first thing we should discuss," said Ben, "is what church should we attend? It should be the church where we will be married in and attend the rest of our live."

"I think before we decide that we have to decide what house we are going to live in," said Jan. "I have decided what I would like but I need your opinions."

"Annie and I would like it to be Ben's house. We know that it is bigger than you need but it is so beautiful, and it was designed and built by our dad," said Diana.

"Does anyone want to discuss this further," asked Ben? No one responded. "All that agree that we live in my home please raise your hand." They all raised their hand.

"With that agreed on," said Jan "I think the church we go to should be the church we will be married in and the one we will be going to the rest of our life. After we move into Ben's house the church we are presently going to will be much farther than Ben's church."

"I guess that means that tomorrow morning you will be at my house by nine thirty so we can all go to church together."

"Agreed," said Jan. Soon after, the pizza was delivered, and they all had a nice dinner.

Sunday morning after the service Ben introduced Jan to the minister. They discussed the coming wedding. The minister told them that the spring was already pretty full. He told them to find a venue for the wedding and then get together with him. If the church is not available he could marry them at the place they find to celebrate. After they left the church they went to Ben's house for a steak dinner. Ben explained that this was his custom for Sunday lunches. He has been doing this since he got his own house. After lunch Jan asked Ben to sit with her and discuss the coming wedding. "Honey," she said. "I have a list of things we have to do. I need you to do some since in a week I will be teaching and as a teacher I can't just leave. I will try to do as much as I can before I have to go to work. I will get a nice place for the rehearsal dinner and the wedding celebration. Until that is done, we can't plan anything. Perhaps in the mean time we can get information on a band and flowers for the church. If I can't get a venue before I go to work you have to follow through with some of these requirements. Do you think this is possible?"

"I will do whatever you ask me to do," responded Ben. "I told my dad that I can't take over the business until after the honeymoon. Until then I will only do architectural work and I will do that at home. So you see I will be available as needed."

"Great," said Jan. "I am going to see about ordering some invitational cards. Do you want to have a say in the selection?"

"No," Ben answered. "I don't know anything about that. I'm sure the sales lady will help you. Besides you have very good taste in things like that. It would be easier for you to just go whenever you get a chance."

"Fine," said Jan. "I felt I had to ask."

"It was Wednesday at Ben's house for dinner that Jan pulled them all together after they finished the desert.

"Look guys," said Jan. "I have something to tell you. I have been trying since Sunday to find a place to hold our wedding celebration. I called six different places and could not find anything. They had no dates available after you girls get back from school. They have room either before you girls get out or way down at the end of August.

"So what do we do," asked Ben?

"I do have one possibility. The Hilton near your home, Ben, has a ballroom available on Saturday

December 29." For a few minutes no one said a word. They were all stunned. Then Ben looking at his calendar spoke.

"Christmas this year is on Tuesday. That would make it four days after Christmas. Wow," was the last words that Ben uttered.

"The question, if you accept this, is will the girls be home during that time. Do you girls have any Ideas?"

"I know that I will get Christmas off," said Diana, "But will we have time to get things like our bridesmaid dresses in time?"

"I will get time off if I have to cut classes," said Annie. As for the dress, I will go with my jeans if necessary."

"I'm sure your college will give you Christmas off. For your dresses, I can take care of that. All you have to do is come for the final fitting. Therefore," said Jan. "Is this alright with every one?" Everyone accepted the date with joy.

The weeks went by like they were days. Everything worked out perfectly. Ben's family came up to meet Jan as soon as they received the invitation card. Ben asked Jim, his brother-in-law to be his best man. Jim accepted with joy. They had a very delightful evening.

Before they knew it, it was the Friday before the wedding. The Hilton set up the ballroom for the rehearsal dinner. The rehearsal and dinner went very well. Jan's parents came from California to be at Jan's rehearsal dinner and wedding. Ben loved them at first sight.

They became very close as did Jan and Ben's family. After the dinner, Hilton changed the ballroom for the celebration with table as specified by Jan. From that moment on Ben was in a trance. He was barely aware of all that went on the next day. Thanks to the girls everything went well. Ben came out of his trance for a moment when he saw Jan coming down the aisle with her father. She was the most beautiful sight he had ever seen. The only thing Ben remembered after that was the Pastor announcing that they were husband and wife. At the wedding celebration Ben was in a cloud the whole evening. When he came out of his cloud he found that they were on the way to Bella valley Lodge where Jan had made reservations, at Ben's suggestion. She made sure she got the bungalow they had spent time earlier in the year. As they entered the bungalow Ben took a deep breath.

"I understand that they have a few winter activities," said Ben, "like sleigh rides, ice skating on the pond behind the tennis courts, and during bad weather they have activities inside, such as dances in the ballroom, and Ping-Pong tables, if you can't play tennis outside." "Yes they do," said Jan. "we may go on one or two but most of the activities I want are inside activities."

"You know," said Ben, "That ticket I won was a ticket to romance." "I think it was also a ticket to my heart," added Jan. Ben was about to say something but Jan's passionate kiss stopped him. The kiss reminded Ben what Jan meant by inside activities.

The End

PREDESTINED ROMANCE

The day was rather cool this early in the spring. gino and Terrie usually sat on his or her front porch. Sometimes they would go for a bicycle ride down the street to the park and back. most of the time, they would stay around the house. They would in general enjoy each other's company. Sometimes they would tell each other funny stories or a joke they had recently heard. Because it was a little chilly they decided to sit in the back seat of gino's father's car, that was parked in the drive way.

"This is a lot cozier," said gino. "We are alone and can do anything we like."

"What are you thinking," asked Terrie.

"I think we should experiment about the thing we saw in the movie." gino and Terrie had been going to the movie almost every Saturday afternoon. They had permission from their parents and took advantage of the permission. Terrie was his next door neighbor. They were both about twelve years old. They were allowed to play with each other but had to be in for dinner. After dinner they were not allowed to go out again. That afternoon they had gone to the theater as usual. most of the time the theater showed a movie that was a mystery or a cowboy movie. This afternoon they had a romantic movie. During the movie the actor and the actress hugged and kissed each other several times.

"I wonder why they kiss on the lips," asked Terrie.

"I don't know," said gino. "They must taste something good because they seem to really enjoy it."

"It can't be leftover food," said gino in jest. "They haven't eaten anything lately." Terry laughed at gino's answer.

"I wonder what they get out of it," said Terrie. "There is only one way to find out," said gino.

"And how is that?" said Terry, actually knowing what gino had in mind.

"I think we have to try it," said gino. He then bent over and kissed Terry on the lips. He held it for a while with his arms around her. After they their lips parted, gino kept his arms around her.

"You can let me go now," said Terrie. "What did you think?" "Your lips were warm and very soft," said gino. "It was very nice. I enjoyed having my arms around you the most."

"You're being silly," said Terrie. "I didn't get the feeling that the guy in the movie said that he felt."

"And what was that," asked gino? "I don't remember what he said."

"He said that he got butterflies in his belly and a lump in his throat," said Terrie. "Did you feel that?"

No," said gino. "But that is just a movie. They say anything to give a verbal account of his feelings. It is just a made up story. I don't believe that happens with real people."

"Well I think it does," said Terrie. "I have heard of it before." "Well let's try it again," said gino. "maybe you have to do it several times before you get that feeling."

"No way," said Terrie. "I don't think friends should do that." "We are more than friends," said gino. "You are my girlfriend.

A boy is allowed to kiss his girlfriend."

"I am not your girlfriend," said Terrie. "You are my neighbor. We are only friends."

"Why do you say that," asked gino? "Don't you want to be my girlfriend?"

"I have two reasons that I am not your girlfriend," said Terrie. "First we are too young to have that kind of a relationship. Secondly, my mother told me that you are moving in about two week and are never coming back."

"That is not true," said gino. "I will be back. I am a born citizen of this country. Even if my parents want to stay in Sicily I would come back when I get older, especially if I had a girlfriend that loved me and I loved her."

"First of all," said Terrie, "I am not that girl. I don't feel that way about you. Then, I think you will forget me two days after you have left."

"I love you," said gino sounding heart broken. "Don't you have any feeling for me?"

"I'm sorry gino."

"Well I want to inform you of one thing," said gino. "You are breaking my heart. I will never let a girl break my heart twice. I could never trust her. So be forewarned, if you let me go now you will never get another chance."

"I'm sorry,"repeated Terrie."I don't want any kind of relationship at this time." Feeling very sad, gino left the car and disappeared into his home.

Two weeks later gino, his sister mary, and his mother left for New York where they were to board a ship to Italy. gino's father stayed behind. The plan was that they were to see how gino and mary accepted the different temperature and living conditions. They would wait a few months and if all went well, gino's father would sell the house and joined them in Sicily. They were to live there the rest of their lives. When they got to New York they were met by a distant relative of gino's mother. It was who gino called Uncle Alfonzo and Aunt

Lina. They lived in Passaic New Jersey. They came to New York to wish them a happy voyage. once they got under way, gino explored the ship. He found a very nice swimming pool at the rear deck. He also found a play room that had ping pong tables and card tables. He enjoyed most of them during the trip. What however, he enjoyed the most is the Bingo games in the afternoon and the stage play or movie in the evening after a fantastic dinner. gino enjoyed the trip very much until they got to the Rock of gibraltar. Through that pass gino got very sea sick. Twice he almost threw up his meal. For the two days it took to go through the pass gino did not eat anything. Soon they were at the port of Naples. From there they took the ferry boat to Palermo. There they were met by uncle Toto and grandpa Salvatore. Toto, gino's mother's baby brother, was two years younger than gino. It was hard for gino to think of him as his uncle. Toto agreed for gino to just call him Toto. When they got to Barrafranca, there was a great party to welcome them. gino couldn't remember any ones name the next day. The only names he remembered were Toto, grandpa Salvatore, grandma Stellina, and a cousin names gaetano. Every one called him Tano. There were several young girls in the family but gino was not interested in them due to his experience with Terrie. The next few days were filled with visiting several family members. There was Aunt maria and Aunt Rosa that were closer than the rest. They were gino's father's sisters. They spent a lot of time with them. gino however spent a lot of time with Toto. Tano had to help his father on the farm. gino only saw him sometimes in the evening and on the week end. However Toto was sometimes free during the day.

"Don't you have to go and help grandpa with the farming," asked gino?

"He needs me most in the early spring and in the fall," answered Toto, "the rest of the year my sister's husbands are enough help." When Toto was out helping his father gino spent a lot of time with his cousins Peppino who was gino's father's sister's son. When Peppino was out helping his father gino spent a lot of time with his female cousins Angelina and Sarafina. He would play cards with them. one day when he was alone he built the model airplane he brought from ohio. The girls had fun chasing it when gino sent it flying from the third floor terrace. gino had a good time during these first weeks in Barrafranca.

One day when Toto had some free time he called on gino. "By the way," said Toto, "Do you know how to ride a horse?" "I have been on a horse a couple of times," answered gino. "Why do you ask?"

"I asked my dad if he could spare a horse for you to ride," said Toto.

"That would be great," said gino. Although, he hadn't ridden a horse since he was five at a carnival, how hard could it be he thought? That afternoon they went riding into the country side. gino had no problem. He was able to handle the horse after about an hour riding. "I want to take you up to the mountains," said Toto. "The scenery up there is fabulous."

"The scenery here is fabulous," said gino. He had never in his life even dreamed about anything like this. They went horse riding at least twice a week.

All good things eventually come to an end. It was about the end of July when gino's grandfather pulled gino aside.

"Gino honey, I'm going to need Toto now at the farm more often. We are getting ready for the summer planting. I also have something for you. Your mother and father would like you to have a future other than farming. So I have set up a deal with the local carpenter, Senior Francisco moreno. He will teach you how to be a carpenter. You start tomorrow morning at eight." gino had no choice, however the idea did sound very interesting.

Gino started to help Senior moreno at first by just sanding down furniture that Senior moreno had built. Later he gave him more interesting work like making measurement and cutting parts of a piece of furniture. one of the most interesting jobs that gino loved was the times that he was needed to installing doors, kitchen cabinets, and other installations where gino's help was really needed. By the end of the summer gino was doing carpenter work. His last job was the building a casket for an eight year old girl that had passed away from a heart problem. gino did all the fine trim creating and installing.

At the end of August gino was told that he had been registered at the city school. on September third, gino was taken to school by his mother and was admitted to a fourth grade class. After that first day, gino having learned the way went back and forth to school by himself. He learned quickly that the Italian teachers were not as lenient as the American teachers. About the fourth day in school he asked the student next to him a question. The instructor hit him on his hand with his ruler. gino learned not to talk during class. It was a couple of days later as gino was leave school that he noticed a girl with long black hair leaving the school at the same time as he. At first glance gino felt paralyzed. She was so beautiful, graceful, and pleasant. He had never seen a girl like this before. When she spoke to the girl friend she was walking with, her voice sent a chill down his spine. She then turned toward gino.

"Ciao" she said looking at gino. "You are the American aren't you?" she said in a sweet Italian language. gino was in a state of shock. He felt a strange feeling in his stomach. He found it hard to speak.

"Hi" he said in English.

"Welcome to our city," she said as she walked away. gino had never before felt the way he was feeling at this moment. He was enjoying the moment more than he had ever before. However, it was a mixed feeling. He found that he wasn't thinking strait. He hated the lack of control he had. He loved to look at her but he wanted to be as far away from her so that he wouldn't feel so awkward. From that day on, he stayed in the class room longer than necessary fooling around with his notebook. He always wanted her to leave before him. He could always see her down the road and he would slow down so not to catch up with her. When he didn't see her he felt bad. He liked to look at her. Weeks went by and the pattern never changed. He would always look at her but always keep his distance. one of his class mates named Paulo, who often walked down the road with him notices gino's reluctance to be near the girl who was most of the time ahead of them. He noticed that when the girl stopped to talk to someone that gino stopped and hesitated to continue down the road.

"What is going on" said Paulo. "Did you have a fight with Anna maria?"

"Who," asked gino? "I don't know any one by that name." "She is the girls with the long black hair that you have been avoiding for the past few weeks," said Paulo.

"To tell you the truth," confessed gino, "she makes me feel awkward. I don't know what it is but I don't like the feeling."

"My goodness," said Paulo. "You are falling in love with Anna maria."

"How could that be," said gino? "I don't even know her. I just said hello once when we first started school."

"It doesn't matter," said Paulo. "Love is like the flu. You can catch it any time."

The rest of the year went by with nothing changing. gino kept his distance but always enjoyed looking at her. As he thought of her he remembered what Terrie had said to him, about the butterflies in the belly and the lump on his throat. After analyzing his feelings he accepted that what he felt for Anna marie was that. What, he wondered, was, what did it all mean?

The holidays went by quickly.They didn't have a Halloween, but they had a feast they called Carnevale. People, who want to celebrate it, dress up in costumes with masks and travel the neighborhood. The houses that celebrate the feast have their doors wide open with loud music playing. gino dressed up with a mask and went to a couple of houses and danced with some of the young girls that traveled the circuit. gino went to just two houses. He was embarrassed because he was recognized as the Americano.

The next holiday was Christmas. gino loved this holiday because, except for the lack of a Christmas tree, it was the same as it was in the USA. New Year's Day consisted of a large dinner with all the family around you. gino did not see Anna marie at any time during the holidays. The rest of the winter went by with only an occasional rain that made it different. gino still kept away from Anna marie. He enjoyed seeing her at a distance.

It was early in march when things turned upside down. gino was just getting up to go to school.

"Get up," said gino's mother. "Pack your suitcase we have to get out of here in a hurry."

"What is happening?" said gino being very confused with all the excitement. He became aware that many of their relatives were running around outside.

"Your dad has requested that we come home. There is a war going on out here and your dad says that we will be safer in America."

"Do we have to leave right away," asked gino?

"Yes," answered his mother. "I was lucky to get a car this morning. most of the few cars that are here are on a trip or taken up by other people. He will be here any minute. He is only available this morning. He is busy this afternoon. There are only a couple of cars available and they are usually busy driving business people to Palermo or Catania. So hurry and get ready. He wants to leave as soon as he gets here." They were in such a rush that it was very difficult to say goodbye to those that showed up. Too many were out working on their farm. As soon as the car arrived gino and his mom got into the car. There was no passenger seat in the front. That was where the business men placed their suitcase and brief cases. After they placed their suitcases in the front, gino's mother got in the rear seat and gino's sister mary got in and sat on her mother's lap. gino was ready to get in the back seat with them when a man came up to the car.

"Please let me share the car with you," he asked."I'm an America and I would like to get out of this country. You have the only car available. Please I have to get out of here."

"There is no room for another person," said gino's mother. "The trip is about a four hour trip. It would be difficult to have another person in the car."

"Please," said the man, "You can't leave me here. Please, I will sit in the back seat with your son on my lap."

"Gino is not a small boy," said gino's mother. "You will be hurting after four hours. Do you think you can take that?"

"If I have to sit on the roof I have to get to Naples before tomorrow afternoon when the ship sails. If I don't get there in time I will never leave this country. There is no other ship scheduled to leave for America."

"Hurry up and make up your mind," said the driver. "I'm going to leave is ten seconds."

"Alright," said gino's mother. "I guess I can't leave you here." The man quickly pulled gino out of the back seat, got in and then pulled gino on to his lap. No sooner that was done the driver took off.

"My name is Joseph Banio," said the man introducing himself. "my name is Catharina Corino. This is my daughter mary, and the boy on your lap is gino. my husband's name is Joseph." She added her husband's name to make sure mr. Banio understood that she was married. They were on the main road for just a few minutes when Joseph requested a favor.

"Please," he asked. "Could you just go one block out of your way so that I could say goodbye to my family. I won't even get out of the car. I will lower the back window and say good bye. I didn't get a chance to say goodbye because I wasn't sure I could get a ride."

"But you were carrying a suitcase," said gino's mom. "Didn't they see you packing it?"

"I had it packed two days ago, when I started to look for a driver," responded Joseph. The driver didn't object. He got directions from him and soon stopped in front of the house of Joseph's family. The people of the house came running out to say goodbye to him. After the adults said their goodbyes they pushed a little boy through the window. He was crying as he hugged Joseph. gino was disturbed because putting the boy through the window caused gino to move his head which was in the way. Never in a million years did he expect what happened next. After they pulled out the little boy they pushed a little girl through the open window. It was Anna marie. gino almost yelled out. Her face came within an inch of gino's face. gino was in a confused state. on the one hand he felt such a strong feeling that he wanted to hug her and kiss her. on the other hand he wanted to get away as fast as he could. The feeling he was having was almost more than he could bear. He turned his head away as far as he could. When he turned back to see if she was gone he found that they were looking straight into each other's eyes. She was looking at him with tears in her eyes. She had such a loving look and her eyes were calling out to him. He wanted to kiss her so badly. As they started to pull her out she was tilted so that her lips were about an inch from his. gino froze. However, before he could recover they pulled her out and they were on their way to Palermo. gino felt sad, but in a way he felt relieved. As they drove gino started to talk to Joseph.

"Mr. Banio," he started. "What is going on? No one told me why we are in such a hurry to leave Italy."

"I know," said Joseph. "I was told that germany has started to attack France and that Italy was ready to join germany to fight against France. If Italy gets involved we will be stuck here."

"Is that so bad," asked gino?

"I believe that this country will be bombed by England and if America gets in the war it will be a world war. We will all be safer in America. I don't believe that germany or Italy will have the capability to bomb America." gino was satisfied with the answer and the subject was not brought up again.

When they got to Palermo they were driven to the water front where they got on a ferry boat and were soon in Naples. From there they walked down to the harbor where the ocean liner Conti di Savoia was docked. once they got aboard and got settled Joseph came to gino's cabin.

"Catherina," he said. "Why don't we go looking around Naples? The ship will not sail until tomorrow morning."

"I don't think so," said gino's mother. "I'm very tired from the trip.

Besides I'm not in to that kind of entertainment."

"Do you mind then if I take gino with me," said Joseph. "I could use the company. Besides, when will he ever get the chance to see Italy again?"

"Do you want to go," Catherine asked gino? "I would love that," answered gino.

"Go ahead then," said gino's mother. "Be careful. When do you think you will return?"

"I'm not sure," said Joseph. "If we like what we see we may just have dinner in a local restaurant." With that said they left. Joseph took gino all over Naples. The first thing he did is buy gino a gelato. At about six they had a small pizza each. They returned to the ship about nine. This was repeated every time the ship docked and was scheduled to stay several hours. gino will never forget his tour of milan. Joseph took him to the marble Pit. It was a hole in the ground that looked like the grand Canyon. gino looked down through the wire fence that surrounded the pit. At the bottom he saw a train. It looked so small that it looked like gino's toy train.

The trip lasted eight days. After the ship left the Italian area it stopped at monte Carlo in France, and two ports in Africa. After going through the Strait of gibraltar they stopped at Casablanca. on the way across the Atlantic they stopped at an island. It was on the eighth day that Joseph call Catherine and gino out on the ship's deck.

"Look," he said pointing out into the water. "We are sailing under the Statue of Liberty. We are almost home."

"Hooray," yelled gino. "This is the second time I have sailed under the Statue of Liberty. I promise myself that someday I will come and climb up to the crown of the stature." After landing they turned to Joseph. gino felt bad. He loved Joseph like his own dad. With tears he hugged Joseph and they said goodbye. gino and his mother spent two days with Uncle Alfonzo and Aunt Lina. gino's mother wanted to go home. After they got home gino's mother took him to see the school principal as to where they should place him. Because he had gone to school in Sicily they placed gino in the same class he was in when he left for Sicily. gino did not go back to Terry. She tried to get close to him again but gino always had an excuse to be somewhere else. one day Terrie's older sister Carmela cornered gino.

"Why don't you give Terrie another chance," she asked?" I'm sure you have noticed that she is crazy about you."

"I gave her a chance once," said gino. "She broke my heart. I will not give her another chance to break it again."

The days flew by and gino was soon in high school. gino had not dated any girl since they got back from Sicily. He was in his senior year when he met Caroline. He liked her very much. She was very good looking and was a lot of fun. gino started to date her. much of the time they went on a double date with his buddies Nick or Jim. Caroline didn't like that. She wanted to be alone with gino. gino and Carol became known as sweethearts. gino didn't feel the stomach butterflies like he did with Anna marie in Sicily but after a while he began to believe that it was a crazy thing that happens only to kids. gino took Carol to his graduation dance. They had a great time and gino began to believe that she was the one true love. However he wished that she would not be so wild.

In 1941 America had been brought into World War 11 by the bombing of Pearl Harbor by the Japanese. gino graduated in the spring of 1945. Therefore, immediately after graduation, gino was drafted into the army. He served his Basic Training in West virginia, and after a week at home was sent to the Philippines. His unit followed the marines into Luzon. After the war was declared over, gino's unit was deployed to clean up Corregidor. There were Japanese units in Corregidor that were not aware that the war was over. After gino got enough points that were given solders with enough time and action, he was shipped to California where he was discharged. He telephone Carol and told her he was coming home. He didn't call his parents. He wanted to surprise them. When his train arrived in Cleveland gino was surprised to see Carol there.

"What are you doing here," said gino. "How did you know what train I was coming in on?"

"I have my ways," said Carol. "I thought we should talk before you went home."

"What do you want to talk about?" asked gino having no idea what she wanted.

"I want to talk about us," answered Carol. "I think we should talk about the next step in our relationship.

You have been gone almost two years and I missed you."

"I missed you too," said gino. "What are you really talking about?" "Alright," said Carol. "I guess I have to say it. I know that this is too soon but we have to discuss this now. When you get home it will be a while before we can be together. They will be celebrating your coming home for days I'm sure."

"What are you talking about?" asked gino. "Let's not beat around the bush. Say what you want."

"Alright," said Carol getting up her courage. I want us to get married."

"Wow," said gino. "Do we have to plan that right now? I love you very much and I think some day we can get married. But why do we want to discuss it now?"

"Because I want to get married as soon as you get settled home and get your parent to help with the planning."

"Sweetheart," said gino. "I can't get married now. First of all I don't have a job and I can't support a wife. Secondly I want to go to college and get an engineering degree. I won't be ready to get married for at least four years."

"I can't wait that long," said Carol. "I need a man in my life. I have a good job. I can support us until you graduate and get a job. I would love to do that."

"I'm sorry," said gino. "I have to think about it. give me a few days and we will talk about it then." Carol dropped gino at his home and left with a sad look on her face.

Gino dated Carol for the next couple of weeks. He could tell that she wasn't the same girl he knew. She often brought up the marriage idea. She wanted to know what he had decided. gino kept putting her off.

one day when gino called Carol for a date, her mother answered.

"Hello," said gino. "may I speak with Caroline," he asked. "She is not home," answered her mother. "Haven't you heard?

She and george ran off and eloped." gino just hung up the phone. He was heartbroken, but at the same time relieved. He realized that Carol must have been dating george while gino was in the service. She had two men on the hook. At least gino was her number one in her book.

When the fall came gino enrolled at Cleveland State University, in the Electronics Engineering School. He didn't date for the next two years. It was in his third year that he met Carla. He met her when his friend Ray, who was home for the holiday from college, was asked to deliver a package to Carla. It was from a school mate of Ray's who was a high school friend of Carla. gino went with him to keep him company. They had planned on going to a movie afterwards. Carla had a room at the Salvation Army Student Housing apartments for woman. They met in the lounge. visitors were not allowed up in the rooms. The moment that gino saw Carla, he was in love. He was floating in air he felt some tingling in his belly. It was not the same as he felt for Anna in Sicily, but perhaps that only happens to twelve year olds. He could hardly talk to her. He was so shook up. When they left the building, what had happened to gino was very obvious to Ray.

"She got to you didn't she," asked Ray?

"What are you talking about," asked gino acting innocent? "I've known you since high school. I can tell when you are not yourself."

"Is it's that obvious," asked gino?

"Yes, responded Ray. "I have never seen you so bedazzled. Why don't you call her tomorrow and see if she was bedazzled too."

"Do you think she was impressed with my stupid reaction" said gino? "All I could say was, hello, nice to meet you. I hope you are fine. How could I have sounded more stupid?"

"Well," answered Ray. "I never met her before so I don't know what her natural reaction would be in meeting new people, but I thought that she seemed a little uneasy also when she looked at you." "What do I have to lose," said gino. "I will call her tomorrow"

The next day was Thursday and gino thought that that would be a good time to call and ask for a date on Friday evening. That was because neither had the excuse of school the next day. At about six that evening gino called Carla's number and a woman answered.

"Salvation Army Student Apartments," she said. "Whom do you want to talk to," she asked.

"I would like Carla's room please," asked gino. The woman dialed and gino heard a phone ringing. A few minutes later a girl answered.

"Hello," she answered. gino recognized her voice. Her voice thrilled him.

"Hi," he answered. "This is gino Corino. We met yesterday." "of course," she answered. "You came with Ray when he delivered the package to me. How are you? What can I do for you?" "I'm sorry we couldn't stay longer. Ray had someplace else to go.

I would like to have stayed longer to get to know you."

"Yes that would have been nice," Carla answered. "I'm from New mexico and don't know too many people in this area."

"Well how about you and I going out tomorrow evening," asked gino. "We can go to dinner and get to know each other." gino held his breath waiting for her answer. He didn't have to wait long because she answered quickly.

"I would like that," said Carla. "I haven't been around this area at all."

"Then perhaps after dinner I can take you downtown and show you all the nice places here in Cleveland. maybe we could go to a movie or stop at a bar for a drink."

"That would be perfect," said Carla. "Tomorrow is Friday. I will only go out on weekends. my education is my top priority. Also I don't drink. We could go to the museum or someplace like that"

"Well if we eat at about six and go to a movie downtown, we would be out about ten. We could go to an Ice cream parlor and have a Sundae."

"I think on our first date," said Carla, "we should delay at the restaurant and have an extra cup of coffee and get to know each other. I should tell you that I have to get in before twelve. After twelve the doors are locked. The guard has to let me in. If I'm late three times, they inform my parents."

"You will not believe how glad I am to hear that," said gino. "That tells me a lot about you. Also I'm glad to hear that you don't drink. I usually go to a tavern down town and order a beer. I leave most of it there when I leave. I go there because they have very good dance music. I love to dance."

"I love to dance also," said Carla. "We will have to go there some day."

"You will never guess how happy that makes me," said gino. "I'm happy mostly because you feel we will have other dates."

"You never know," said Carla shyly.

Gino spent Thanksgiving and Christmas with his parents. It was too soon to take Carla home to meet his parents. However, only a few weekends went by when gino and Carla weren't together. gino took her to all the nice restaurants and many evening to the movies. mostly after dinner they ended the evening dancing at the tavern. gino's greatest moment was when he took Carla home and she let him kiss her goodnight. on Saturdays when the weather was nice he took her to places like the Cleveland zoo and once to the History museum. They became an item to their friends. It was the weekend before New Years that while gino was driving Carla home that he mentioned that he never felt for any one the way he felt about her. Carla just looked at him and smiled. This encouraged gino so that the next weekend as they parked in front of her place that he confessed to her.

"Carla," he started, "I think I am falling in love with you. "I have already fallen in love with you," Carla confessed.

"I should clarify my statement," said gino. "I'm not falling in love with you. I've been in love with you since I first met you. When I first saw you, I got butterflies in my stomach and a lump in my throat. I'm surprised you didn't notice it."

"I noticed it," said Carla. "That is what interested me." "When did you realize that you loved me," asked gino?

"It was on the day that we were coming home from downtown and you said that you never felt for anyone the way you felt for me. I knew from the great joy it brought me that I was in love with you. I think we are talking too much," said Carla as she put her arms around gino and pulled him in for a passionate kiss. The rest of the evening they kissed until Carla almost missed the entrance time into the building.

Gino and Carla dated most weekends. When the weather got bad Carla wouldn't let gino pick her up. They had to wait for a better weekend. The winter went by faster than they wanted it go. It was soon time for Carla to go home for the summer. Carla to gino's disappointment wouldn't let gino drive her to the airport. They said goodbye when gino dropped her off after their last date. gino missed her very much. They wrote each other by what they called chain letters. As soon as gino got a letter from Clara he would write back. As soon as Carla got gino's letter she would write back. This went on all summer. Soon it was fall. gino would start school the first week of September. gino expected information from Carla so that he would pick her up at the airport. About a week before he was to start school he got a call from Carla.

"Hi gino," she said. "Are you ready to start dating me again?" "I'm so ready," said gino. "What time will your plane get in so that I can pick you up and we could go on our first date of the year?" "Silly," said Carla. "Today is Friday and you should pick me up at six as you usually do. It is now five and you have an hour to get dressed and pick me up."

"You are not at the airport," asked gino?

"No," said Carla. "I came in yesterday. I had to be here this morning so that I could register for my classes. So are you coming? I have the same room as I had last year"

"I'll be there in an hour give or take a few minutes," said gino. He had just gotten home from school and was dressed well enough to go to pick her up. He had to inform his mother and get some cash from his desk. gino's mother was ready to prepare supper. She was glad that gino told her so that she could trim back what she was cooking.

Gino got to the apartment building five minutes to six. As he entered the building he felt like he was reliving the past. Carla came down as soon as she was informed that he was there. As soon as she saw gino she threw herself into his arms and gave him a passionate kiss. She didn't care who was watching.

"I'm missed you so much," said Carla and landed another kiss on gino. After they parted gino grabbed her by the arm and lead her toward the door.

"I missed you too," said gino. "I think I missed you more than you missed me."

"Why do you say that," asked Carla?

"Well, because you were in a different location, where you didn't know me," answered gino. "Here every place I went reminded me of you."

"You have a point," said Carla.

"Anyway, where would you like to go for dinner," asked gino? "I would like to go to a place that not only has good food but also has beautiful music," said Carla. "I would like to go where we could dance. I would like your arms around me with music."

"That pretty well has limited the place to go," said gino. After dinner, he took her to the place that they had always gone before to dance. They would buy a beer and leave most of it when they left. They just went there to dance. gino loved having his arms around her. Everything went back to the way it was the year before. on one of their dates, when they were parked in front of her building, after a passionate kissing session, gino stopped and faced her eye to eye. "Carla," he started. "You know that I love you very much. Will you marry me?"

"Yes," said Carla, being aware all along at what gino had in mind. "Yes, I will marry you, a million times yes."

"I don't have the money to buy you the ring that you deserve," added gino. "Until I get a job and can afford one I would like you to wear this dime store ring." gino put in on her finger and they went back to kissing.

When Thanksgiving came gino, having told his mother about the engagement, asked his mother if he could invite Carla.

"Of course," said his mother. "I am looking forward to meeting her." gino then asked Carla if she would join them for Thanksgiving. She agreed. on Thanksgiving Day, gino picked up Carla and brought her to his parent's house. As she entered the door gino's mother met them there.

"Hello Carla," said gino's mother, "It so nice to meet you." "me too," said Carla. Carla seemed to be very nervous and shy. "Hi," said mary, gino's sister. "Come on in and join the party."

Carla smiled and entered the dining room. There Carla met gino's father. They traded salutations and sat down to eat. The dinner was great. gino carved the turkey. After diner they sat and talked. Later they had desert. Carla didn't eat much desert. She said that she was watching her weight. gino was disappointed that evening. Carla and his family didn't seem to warm up with each other. However gino thought, Carla was shy and this was the first time she had been there. After he dropped her off he returned home and approached his mother.

"Mom," asked gino. "What did you think of Carla?"

"Well it was the first time we met so we didn't get to really know each other. Besides, you know that I would rather you get an Italian girlfriend."

"Come on mom," said gino. "This is important to me. What did you really think?"

"OK," responded his mother. "I think that she is not a very affectionate girl. It will be very hard to get close to her. She seemed to be very independent." Just then mary walked into the room.

"Mary, what did you think of Carla" asked gino?

"She didn't seem very friendly," answered mary. "I tried to bond with her, but she didn't seem to want to. Let's see when she comes here for Christmas."

The next Friday gino picked up Carla to take her to dinner. "What did you think of my family?"

"I was very nervous," said Carla. "I think they were very nice." The next weeks went by as they usually did. They went to dinner on Fridays and Saturday, and after dinner, some times to a movie and once in a while they went dancing. Soon it was Christmas time. Carla was invited to spend Christmas Eve with them. gino said that she could spend the night with them. He told her that she could share the bedroom with his sister mary. She had twin beds in her room. That way she could spend Christmas day with them. Carla told gino that she couldn't make it on Christmas day. She told gino that her parents were going to stop to spend Christmas day with her on their way to Canada to spend time with a relative of her father. gino accepted her answer although at the bottom of his heart he had questions. gino and Carla had talked of marriage. He wondered why Carla and her family hadn't made arrangement to meet him. After all he was going to be their son-in-law after graduation.

The dinner and gift opening on Christmas Eve went great. Because Carla wasn't going to be with them Christmas Day they decided to open their gifts on Christmas Eve instead of Christmas Day. After dinner they sat and talked in the living room to wait for desert. They had decided to open gifts later in the evening. gino looked for Carla and found her in the family room on her phone. At about ten they decided to open gifts. gino's parents gave both their daughter and Carla a beautiful necklace. Carla gave gino's parents two beautiful candle holders. Carla gave gino a beautiful wrist watch. gino gave Carla a leather jacket she had admired one evening in the store window on their way to a movie in down town Cleveland. Everyone in the rest of the family was happy with the gifts they gave each other. The evening went by with joyful and affectionate celebration. Late in the evening gino took Carla home, kissed her good night and wished her a merry Christmas.

The next day gino got up late. His mother had breakfast ready for him. After his sister came down gino cornered them both.

"I would like to know want you girls think of Carla," asked gino. "I know she didn't bond to well with any of you."

"She didn't even try," said mary. "I tried to get a conversation going but she didn't seem interested."

"Yes," said gino's mother. "I think she should have at least bonded with mary. They are approximately the same age."

"So in general, what are you saying," asked gino?

"We only met her twice," said gino's mother. "We don't really know her. my general opinion is that she just isn't a very affectionate person."

"You know her better than we do," said mary. "How nice a person is she to you? You are the one that has to live with her."

"I know what you are saying," said gino. "She seems to love me very much and is a very strong Christian. She is very passionate when we spend a few minutes in the car before she goes inside."

"Well, you know what grandpa used to say," said gino's mother. "He said that passion satisfies the flesh, and affection satisfies the heart. You have to evaluate her attitude with you. She probably is a very sweet person."

"Gino kept this information in his heart. gino had made plans ahead of time at a classy restaurant for New Year's Eve. It had a band and they wanted to dance all night. gino and Carla had a very happy time. At midnight gino gave Carla a very passionate kiss. She reciprocated with a great hug afterwards.

The rest of the winter went by as it had previously. gino picked her up every Friday and Saturday and they went to dinner and most of the time to dance. She loved to dance. gino loved to have his arms around her.

Soon graduation day came and Carla graduated first. gino and his entire family went to her graduation. After graduation Carla began getting ready to go home. She didn't want gino to go with her to the air-port. He said goodbye at the door to her building. They agreed to write chain lettered as they did last summer. Carla said that she would speak with her mother about planning a wedding and inform him of the results in one of her letters. gino kissed her passionately. He had a fearful feeling it would be the last he would give her.

Gino's graduation came a few days after Carla had left. gino's school adviser informed gino that he could attend the graduation activities but the enve-lope he would receive would be empty. gino was told that he needed a few more points to get his graduation degree. With the advisor's help, he set up for a course he would take during the summer. He was assured that after he finished that course he would receive his degree document. The class only had six students. That made it easier since the professor was available to all. gino and Carla when back to writing chain letters as they had done the previous summer. At first her letters told gino how much she missed him. The later letters she discussed what she was doing. one of the letters she told him that she had gotten a job as a music teacher at the local High School. gino wondered why she would get a long term job if she intended to marry him. He asked her in his letter. She never answered, but told him that she was giving piano lessons to young children. She explained how when not teaching she would be selling musical instrument as a sales clerk. Then the letters stopped coming. gino was concerned for her health. He tried to call several times, but no one answered. Finally one day a young girl answered the phone.

"Hello," said a young voice.

"Hello," said gino," can I speak with Carla please?"

"I'm sorry," said the girl, "Carla is at work at the music store. Can I tell her who is calling?"

"Just tell her that a friend from college called." gino then hung up. He knew that Carla wasn't ill. He suspected that Carla's young sister was not supposed to answer the phone. gino was broken hearted. He realized he had been dumped.

The time went by slowly and the class went poorly. gino almost failed the course. He ended up with a D grade. However, he passed and got his degree document. It was the end of July and gino did find a job. However, it would not be available until the end of August. Some of the workers were returning to school and would cause a vacancy. gino wanted some time to relax anyway. He was pretty much over Carla. He was angry with her for not having the decency to call him or at least send a Dear John Letter. one day he was discussing with his sister about where he should spend the next few weeks when his mother broke in.

"I have a good Idea," said gino's mother. "Why don't you go to your Uncle Alfonzo and Aunt Lina? When we arrived in the US we only stayed with then a couple of days because we were in such a hurry to get home. We didn't even meet their son Peppino, since he was out of town when we were there. He is at home now. I'm sure your sister and I would like to go with you," hinted gino's mother.

"You know," said gino deep in thought. "We sailed twice under the Statue of Liberty. I promised that I would someday go up to the top of it. This would give me a chance to do it. Thanks mom. Yes I would love for you and mary to come with me."

On the next Friday they left early on the morning for Passaic, New Jersey. They stopped half way and had lunch at a macDonald Restaurant. It took eight hours to get there. They arrived at Uncle Alfonso house at four in the afternoon. Aunt Lina and her daughter Sarafina were thrilled to see them. Uncle Alfonso got home from work at about five. Peppino came home from shopping just after gino and his family got there. He had gone to buy a musical DvD. He knew that the older women loved that type of movie. They were all so happy to be together. Aunt Lina had prepared a fantastic dinner.

After dinner they all sat down in the family room to talk. The women gathered in one corner to discuss women things. Uncle Alfonso and Peppino sat with gino.

"Tell us about your collage days" asked Uncle Alfonso. "I understand that you graduated with an Engineering Degree." Tell us what you studied and what made you choose that area."

"I studied to be an Electronics Engineer," answered gino. "When I was in high school and I learned about television, I was fascinated by the idea of a picture traveling through the air. So I wanted to know how that was possible."

"Didn't you have other thoughts or ideas on what you wanted to be," asked Peppino?

"I liked to paint pictures on canvas," said gino. "my friend Nick, who actually turned out to be an art teacher, and I would go out in the country with our easel and painted. Nick liked to paint pictures of barns. I like to paint pictures of the trees by a road, river or by a lake. I also liked to draw pictures of animals."

"That sounds like fun," said Peppino. "Do you have a lot of picture hanging from you wall at home?"

"Yes," answered gino. "I have two hanging in our recreation room. I have a picture of a horse hanging in my basement work room. I also have a picture I painted of a row boat on a lake not too far from our home."

"Why didn't you proceed with that gift," asked Uncle Alfonso. "I didn't see a future in art," said gino. "Nick is a much better painter than I, but he hasn't sold very many of his painting. I also loved to write. I started to write a novel. I showed it to Jim a neighbor friend. He laughed at me. That discouraged me from pursuing that course. Now, that is enough about me, what are you guys up to?"

"I work for a builder. I do carpentry work and other things." said Uncle Alfonso. "my only other thing is I like to grow vegetables in my garden. That's my life."

"I know," said gino. "I have tasted many of your delicious backyard creations. How about you Peppino, what are you up to?"

"I work for a builder also. I do mostly inside carpentry work. But that is enough of this. I'm going to take a few days off to show you around town. What would you like to see?"

"I don't know," responded gino. "What do you have that would be interesting?"

"Well we have a History museum, an Art museum, and we have a zoo. What would you like to see first?"

"I will leave that up to you," said gino. "We should ask the women where they will want to go." After talking with the women, they found out that they had plans of their own.

The next day Peppino took gino to the zoo. They had a great time together. Peppino had a very good sense of humor. He made gino laugh at each spot they stopped. The next day after breakfast Peppino asked gino where he wanted to go next.

"You know," said gino. "It probable isn't possible at this visit, but I have had this desire for many years."

"What is it you would like to do," asked Peppino?

"When we went to Sicily, explained gino, "we sailed passed the Statue of Liberty. When we returned we sailed passed the Statue of Liberty. I promised myself that someday I would go up the Statue." "Well that day has finally come, said Peppino. "Tomorrow we will visit the Statue of Liberty."

"That won't be a lot of trouble," asked gino?

"No," responded Peppino, "as a matter of fact, I would like to go up the statue myself. I have never been there."

"I can't believe that," said gino. "You have lived here all of your life and you haven't been up the Statue of Liberty"

"You have lived all your life in Cleveland ohio, and how often have you gone up the Terminal Tower," asked Peppino?

"You are making a good point, said gino. "I have never been up the Terminal Tower."

The next day Peppino prepared to take gino to New York and up the Statue of Liberty. They asked the women if they wanted to go with them. To gino's surprise they all declined. They left early thinking that after the visit to the statue they would see some of New York. The climb up the metal steps inside the statue was much more strenuous then they had suspected. There must have been more than one thousand steps twisted around the inside of the statue. The steps had to go around the metal beams the held together the outer metal sheets that made up the statue. It felt very strange being inside of the structure. It was emptier inside then they had imaged. Part way up they came to the steps that led up the arm to the lantern. However the entrance was blocked. There was a sign that informed that the structure was unstable and too dangerous, and that the structure could not bear the weight of visitors. Finally they reached the top. They walked around the crown. From there they could see all of New York and some of Long Island. They greatly enjoyed the view and the trip around the crown and were thrilled at being there. They spent over an hour enjoying the experience. gino wondered if walking around the top of the Empire State Building would be the same. He decided to ask Peppino.

"Peppino," he asked. "Have you been up the top of the Empire State Building?"

"I did a long time ago," said Peppino. "While we are here we could go up there."

"I would like that, if only to say that I did it," said gino. "I was just wondering if walking around the top of the tower was the same as walking around up here"

"Well, we will see," said Peppino. They stopped at a hot dog stand and had lunch. About an hour later they found themselves on the top of the Empire State Building. They greatly enjoyed the scenery from there. They spent about an hour there looking out over New York.

They were exited at being there and having been able to visit both of these famous places.

"Well," said Peppino, "what do you think?"

"It has been an exciting and wonderful day," said gino. "It has been much greater than I expected."

"Do you think the two places are different," asked Peppino? "Like day and night," said gino. "From the top of the Statue of Liberty, it was like seeing New York from a helicopter or a balloon. You are looking down at all of New York and Long Island. Looking down from the Empire State building we were looking down on famous streets and buildings. I loved looking down on the famous Times Square." After walking around Times Square they decided to have a dinner at an Italian restaurant called Pastaria Italiano. After an excellent dinner, they went home.

The next morning they slept in until ten and then went down for a late breakfast. Uncle Alfonso had already gone to work. Aunt Lina made breakfast for them. She and Sara sat listening to their joyful and exciting time they had experienced the day before. gino could not stop talking about how exciting and wonderful the trip was. After an hour of reliving their trip, gino expressed how satisfied he was for making this trip to New Jersey.

"Well," said Peppino, "I'm so happy that you are enjoying your stay here. You have seen most of this part of New Jersey and a lot of New York. Is there anything else we can do for you?"

"I have one thing I would like to do," said gino. "on our trip back from Sicily, we shared a car with another American. He was trying to get out of Italy from the war as we were. The boat we took home was a slow boat to China as the old saying goes. At every port that the ship stopped, after getting permission from my mother, he took me around the port city. The ship usually stayed at the port for eight hour or more. He always bought me something. Sometimes a pizza, sometimes a gelato, sometimes, if we left early and were there around twelve, he would buy us lunch. When we were in genoa, he took me to see the marble Pits. They were fantastic. They were like the grand Canyon. I understand that he lives around New Jersey. I would love to see him before I go home. I loved him like a second father."

"What is his name," asked Peppino?

"His name is Joseph Banio," responded gino. "I don't know him," said Peppino.

"I have heard of him but I'm not sure of where he lives," added Aunt Lina. "I think he lives around here. However, if he was in Barrafranca, my husband will know him." That evening Peppino brought it up during dinner.

"Dad, we have a question to ask you," said Peppino. He then explained what gino had told him. "His name is Joseph Banio," he added finally.

"Yes I know him," said Peppino's father. "We worked together when I did construction work in New York. He was a brick carrier for a brick layer. That was a few years ago before I went to work for the local builder. New York construction was too hard for me. The company we worked for build only large buildings. If it built houses, I would have stayed with them. I love carpentry work. Sure I know Joey. He doesn't live to far from here. About three years ago he was able to get his family here from Sicily. He tried for about ten years but couldn't bring them over because of the war."

"Where does he live," asked gino getting impatient? The possibility of seeing mr. Banio got him very excited.

"He lives about a couple of miles from here," said Peppino's father. Just wait a minute and I will get you

the address. He left the dining room and a few minutes he returned with a piece of paper in his hand.
"Here, I wrote down the address for you. You just go
north down main Street, past downtown, and turn left
on oak Street. His apartment is only a few buildings on
your right."

"Thank you Uncle Alfonso," said gino gratefully.

The next day was Sunday. In the morning they all
went to church. After the service Aunt Lina made a
light lunch, explaining that she had plans for an extra
special dinner. It was more special than gino had
expected. She made cavatelli with pork neck bones
that gino loved. She also made the special Sicilian
cookies that they all loved. They enjoyed the special
dinner.

Monday morning Uncle Alfonso had to go to work
and Peppino had other plans. After lunch gino decide
to go see if he could fine mr. Banio. He asked the girls
if they wanted to come. Aunt Lina said she was busy
and would see them some other time. gino's Sister
mary and Sarafina, who all called Sara, said they had
other plans. So it turned out that gino and his mother
were the only ones that left to go to mr. Banio's home.
They left after lunch and gino had no trouble finding the address Uncle Alfonso gave him. The building
that mr. Banio lived in was behind two large apartment buildings. There was a narrow alley between the
buildings that led to a four family apartment building.
gino was told that Joseph Banio lived in the bottom
left apartment. As gino got to the end of the alley he
saw Joseph work on the front porch of his apartment.
He saw gino but didn't recognize him. After all he was
twelve years old the last time he saw him. However he
looked behind gino and he recognized gino's mother.
At that he realized who it was in front of her.

"Gino," he yelled out. "Is that you?" before gino could answer Joseph ran up and hugged gino. "It's so nice to see you. What are you doing here?" Before gino could answer him he released gino and hugged gino's mother. "Catharina," he said with joy in his voice. "How are you? It's so good to see you. You look like you looked ten years ago. How do you keep looking so young?"

"You look just the same too," said gino's mother. "It's good to see you too. I understand that you just got your family here from Sicily."

"Yes, about three years ago," said Joseph. "I have been trying for ten years. They wouldn't let them come because of the war." Then turning toward his apartment he yelled out. "Rosa, come out here.

Come out and see who is visiting us." His wife Rosa came running out.

"What is all the noise out here about," she asked? Then seeing gino's mother she yelled out. "Catharina, is that you? Dear Lord, what a great surprise."

"My goodness," said gino's mother. "Are you Rosa Umberto? Are you the young girl that I played with on Foramina street?"

"I was before I got married," responded Rosa with a smile on her face. "I am now Rosa Banio. Any way come on inside and have some good Sicilian coffee." They both went inside leaving gino and Joseph out in front of the porch.

"Let's go sit on the porch. We don't want to go in with the women. It's too hot in there," said Joseph. They both went up on the front porch. gino sat down.

"It's nice and cool here," said gino. "I find New Jersey to be very humid."

"Listen," said Joseph. "Will you pardon me for a few minutes? I've been working on putting up a screen on the porch and I feel very dirty and sweaty. Let me go inside and change. You just sit here. I'll just me a minute." With that he went inside using a private door just about in the middle of his porch. gino wondered how he got to be the only one with a private entrance. It looked like the other apartment had to use the main entrance in the middle of the building. gino was not aware that mr. Banio owned the whole apartment. Just as he was thinking of this a young beautiful young girl came out of the alley and walked toward the apartment building gino was sitting. gino felt a strange feeling in his stomach as he looked at her. He had never felt this way before that he could remember. He realized that he was very attracted to her. She was more beautiful than any other girl he had ever seen. She walked up the stairs towards the main entrance. She stopped at the door and looked at gino. gino noticed a strange look on her face. Seconds later she disappeared thought the main door. It took a little while for gino to get his senses back. He suddenly realized that this whole thing was ridiculous. He lived five hundred miles away. She probably lived in one of the other apartments and that he probably would never see her again. Just then Joseph came back out. He had washed his hands and face and had on nice clean clothes.

"You know," said Joseph. "It's a small world. I never thought we would ever be together again."

"I'm sorry," said gino. "You were so good to me during our trip home. I should have looked for you before this. But I just graduated from college and this is the first time I had a chance to go anywhere." "You do bring back some good memories," said Joseph. "Do you remember the four hour drive we had from Barrafranca to Palermo with you on my lap? That was hard on me. I thought I would never walk again. Remember how we stopped to say goodbye to my relatives?"

"Yes," said gino. "I remember how several people stuck their heads through the window to kiss you goodbye."

"Do you remember," asked Joseph, "the two little children they put through the window to kiss me goodbye?"

"I only remember the pretty little girl," said gino, realizing that the feeling he had back then was because she was very beautiful to him.

"You remember that," said Joseph being surprised. Then he got up and yelled through the door. "Annie come out here I want you to meet someone.

"I just meet mrs. Corino," said Annie as she came out the door. As she stepped out she stopped, looking stunned. gino was more stunned than Annie. He realized that she was the girl that he saw come up from the alley. He got up to greet her and suddenly his heart stopped. He recognized her as the little girl he met in Barrafranca. He recognized the eyes, the sweet lips, and the pretty little nose. She really had not changed that much. Instantly gino knew he was in love. He also realized that the feeling he had in his stomach when he first saw her in Barrafranca were butterflies. He felt them now.

"I'm glad to see you again," gino heard himself say. Then he realized that it was a dumb statement. She couldn't possibly remember the time he first saw her. She was seven years old.

"You look familiar," she said. "I don't remember meeting you." "That's oK," said gino. They both just stood there looking into each other's eyes. Looking at her, gino felt the most delightful and wonderful feeling he had ever had before.

"Father," said Annie finally, "I was talking to mrs. Corino when you called me. I'd better get back and finish the conversation I was having with her." With that she left and as she went through the door she gave a last glance back at gino. Although gino was somewhat relieved, he was not used to the feelings he felt in her. It made him feel sort of weak and losing control being near her. In spite of this he already started to miss her. Joseph then started to talk and although gino paid attention to him he didn't hear a word he said. His mind was totally thinking of Annie. From that moment on gino was in sort of a trance. Later Annie's brother Salvatore came home. He was introduced to gino and mrs. Corino, gino's mother. gino didn't recognize him. gino hardly knew what was going on. Rosa and Joseph invited gino his mother and Uncle's family for dinner. But gino's Aunt Lina was preparing a surprise dinner that evening, but they agreed to come the next day. They had the dinner together the next evening. The apartment had a nice lawn and area in front of it behind the two buildings. Two neighbors who lived down the street from them came after dinner invited by Joseph Banio. one played a mandolin and the other played an accordion. That evening they had a party outside on the lawn. gino only remembers that he got to dance with Annie. The pleasure gino felt was indescribable. This went on several days the rest of the week. Then it was time to go home. gino's sister had been complaining all week. She wanted to go home. gino's mother was also ready to go home. Unknown to gino, the attraction that gino and Annie had for each other had not gone unnoticed by gino's mother and Annie's parents. They sat and discussed how they could get gino and Annie to get to know each other better. They all liked the idea of gino and Annie becoming a couple. However, gino's mother knew better than to suggest a relationship to gino. She knew that he was very much against anything that looked like a pre-arranged marriage. They finally came up with a plan. The night before they were to leave gino's mother pulled him and his sister aside.

"Listen kids," she stated. "I was talking to mr. and mrs. Banio. They were concerned that Annie and Sal had not been anywhere except Passaic, New Jersey. They asked if we would take them with us to ohio and show them some of this great country. I said yes, so they will be going with us tomorrow morning. You guys don't mind do you? It will be your responsibility to show them around ohio."

"No, we don't mind" said mary. "It sounds like it will be a lot of fun."

"How about you gino," asked his mother?

"It's oK," said gino, in a very soft voice. In side he was jumping for joy.

The next morning they left at eight for Cleveland ohio. The three girls sat in the back seat. Sal sat in front with gino. The trip was enjoyable. The girls were having a great time. gino didn't understand all they were talking about but they were laughing most of the time. At about twelve they stopped at mcDonald's for lunch. They all ordered a hamburger. Annie and Sal had only had a hamburger once in their life time. As they ate gino noticed that Annie was looking at him and every time he looked up at her she would look down at her dish. He also liked looking at her. However he found that he did the same thing. Every time he was looking at her and she looked up at him he would look down at his dish. Finally they were back on the road. The girls continued with their cheerfulness. It was about five when they got home to the Corino's house. gino brought Sal to his bedroom. While he was with them Sal would share gino's room. In the meantime mary brought Annie to her bedroom. While she was there she would share marie's bedroom. It was nice since mary's bedroom had twine beds. They were each given a drawer in the dresser to unpack and store their cloths. When they came down gino's mother had made a dinner for them all. When gino's father came home they introduced Annie and Sal to him and they all sat at the table. gino's father said grace and they all ate. During the dinner gino noticed the same thing he had noticed during their luncheon. Every time he would look up at Annie she would look down. gino thought that this was cute. After dinner they talked a while and all went to bed early. They were all very tired from the traveling.

The next two weeks were very enjoyable for all. gino and mary took them to every interesting place in the Cleveland area. Annie would sit in front with gino and Sal would sit in the rear seat with mary. one day they took them to the Art museum. Another day they took them to the Cleveland zoo. Another day they took them to the History museum. Some days they would just go to dinner and then to a movie. It took about a week before Annie was comfortable with gino. on Friday of the first week they went to a restaurant in geauga Lake. on Fridays they had a band that played soft music. They ordered their dinners and then gino asked Annie to dance. She agreed and they danced most of the night. gino loved to have his arms around her. This was the only chance he had to do it.
"You are a beautiful dancer," said gino softly into her ear. "You are too," responded Annie. most of the other evenings the three went out to eat and after dinner they would go to a movie. on Tuesday of the second week they found a place down town called the Arena Ballroom. They only served drinks but they had the best band in the city. gino and Annie liked to dance mostly because that way they could have their arms around each other. They went there twice.

The second time mary and Sal decided not to go with them. In a way gino and Annie were glad. They had not had much time alone together. They spent all night dancing. Late that evening they went home and parked in the driveway. They were reluctant to get out of the car. gino leaned over and looked into Annie's eyes. He was only about an inch away from her mouth. He hesitated awhile and seeing that she didn't pull away he put his arm around her and pressed his lip onto hers. Suddenly it turned into a very passionate kiss. The thrill that gino felt was more than he ever thought was possible. Apparently she felt the same way. gino could feel her trembling. They held the position for several minutes. It was their first kiss. When they parted they hugged each other cheek to cheek. Annie put her mouth near his ear and whispered.

"Gino, I love you."

"I love you too," responded gino. "I think we had better go inside," added gino coming out of his daze. my parents will be angry for keeping you out so late" gino was right. His mother was very upset.

"What am I to tell Annie's parents," asked gino's mother? "You can go tomorrow if you want to, but you must be home by midnight. It will be your last time. Tomorrow is Friday. I want you to stay at home, because they will be leaving Saturday. I think we should spend the last night together." Annie looked sad. gino had never seen her looking sad. She was such an upbeat person, always smiling and being jolly. This was not like her.

"Are you alright," asked gino seeing Annie looking so sad. "I thought you would be happy that you were going home."

"I don't want to go home," said Annie turning and going straight to bed.

The next morning Sal packed his suitcase and helped Annie pack hers. They all had breakfast and gino got set to drive them to the train station. When they were ready to leave Annie hesitated.

"I'm not going home. I will not leave"

"What are you talking about," asked Sal? "We have been here the two weeks. We promised mom and dad that we would only stay two weeks."

"What's the matter," asked gino. "Are you feeling sick?"

"No, I don't want to leave," repeated Annie. "Don't you know how much I love you? I love you. I won't leave you."

"I have really enjoyed your stay here," said gino taken by surprise by her action. "But your father will send an army here to get you if you don't go home."

"Honey," said gino's mother. "You have to go. This is not a permanent goodbye. We will be together again."

"When will I see you again," asked Annie? Then thinking it over, she added. "I will leave on one condition. If you promise me you will come to New Jersey for my birthday on November eleven, I will leave."

"I promise," said gino. "I will see if I could get a day off and fly down and spend your birthday with you and your family, if it is oK with your mom and dad."

"It will be oK with them," said Annie. "I will have them call you to confirm it."

"What day is birthday on," asked gino?

"I think it is on a Friday," answered Annie.

"Good," said gino. "Then I could stay Saturday and go home Sunday morning." With that promise, Annie agreed to leave. The drive to the train station was very quiet. After they got on the train Annie was seen sitting by a window. She had a sad look on her face with tears in her eyes. gino found tears in his eyes.

The next weeks were very hectic. gino started his new job at the end of August. It was a job as a draftsman. He was told he had to start at the bottom. However, they promised him that he would be transferred to the engineering department in about six months. Annie would call gino often. In between gino felt he had to call her. The days went by slowly. Finally it was November ten. gino get on a plane and was picked up by a friend of the family. gino stayed at a hotel that was just a block away. The birthday party they gave Annie was a fantastic affair. gino and Annie danced to the music that was provided by the neighbors that played earlier in the year when gino and is mother were there. They all had a fantastic time. The next day they all rested. Annie was around most of the day helping her mother with the meals and cleaning the kitchen. That evening Joseph, Annie's father, sat next to gino in the living room.

"What do you have in mind for the future," asked Joseph. gino understood what Joseph had in mind.

"I don't know," answered gino. "I just started working a couple of months ago. I don't have any money saved up. I'm not sure where I will live. I will have to discuss this with my parents. I will have them call you after I talk with them." Sunday they all went to church and in the afternoon gino was driven to the airport. Annie hugged gino and wouldn't let go of him. gino had to force himself out of her grip. Soon the plane was in the air. gino had never felt this bad before. When he got home he went back to work but the next day he told his mother his problem.

"Mom," started gino. "I miss Annie so much that I will do anything to be with her. But I don't have any money and where would we live if we got married?"

"Don't worry about that," said his mother. "Do you really love her and want to marry her?"

"Yes, said gino. "I want to very much. I thought that Carla was my true love, but I never had the feelings for Carla that I have for Annie" gino's mother then got on the phone and called Joseph Banio. After a small conversation she turned to gino.

"They are delighted at the idea. Now go to our cousin Frankie and buy an engagement ring. They are coming here for the New Year celebration. They can't come for Christmas. They have other plans." gino did as his mother directed him. He got her a very beautiful ring. He charged it to his credit card. He wasn't sure how he was going to pay for it but he was given a fantastic discount.

Mister and mrs. Banio with their daughter arrived on Thursday afternoon. gino's father picked them up at the train station. Sal did not come with them. New Years was on Friday. To celebrate the holiday gino gave Annie the ring. gino doesn't remember asking her to marry him. It had all been arranged by the family. The time went by too quickly. mr. Banio informed them that they had tentatively selected may tenth as the wedding day. The rest of the visit went by with great joyfulness. gino's mother had a phonograph machine and played several very romantic songs. gino and Annie got to dance often. Like all good things it all came to an end too soon. But the Banio's left with great joy looking forward to the wedding day.

"The days seemed like weeks and the week seemed like months. Finally may was around the corner. His best friend Nick agreed to come with him to New Jersey and be his best man. The trip was very memorable. There were four cars on the trip. They all followed gino in his car. gino called it the wedding parade. They got to Passaic about five. Joseph and Rosa had a great dinner ready for them. From that evening on gino was in a haze. He walked around as if he was in a trance. He remembers that he and his parents spent the night in a motel around the corner. He remembers Annie walking up the aisle. She looked so beautiful. He couldn't believe that she was willing to marry him. gino hardly remembers any of the service. He remembers telling her he loved her and would spend the rest of his life making her happy. He remembers her saying that she loved him and that she would respect and obey him. He remembered this because he thought the words obey was usually not promised any more in the rituals. He remembers the priest saying the words,

"I now pronounce you husband and wife." After that everything was like a dream. He remembers the next morning having breakfast with Annie's parents. None of the guests were around. It was on the way to Florida on the highway, when gino snapped out of his trance and came to real life. He suddenly realized that he was married and heading for his honeymoon. He looked at the passenger seat. There sitting in the seat next to him was the little girl with long black hair that he had met in Sicily over ten years ago. She still gave him butterflies in his stomach.

The End

ROMANCE ON THE BEACH

Andrew sat in his family room not sure of what to do. School was out for the summer. He would like to take a vacation. He would like to take a trip somewhere. Normally for the summer he would work for a friend who owned an auto repair shop. one time he had traveled withhis parents to Sweden where they stayed with relatives of his father. once they went to Italy. Andrew's mother was Italian. most of the summers they would visit Andrew's Aunt Nicolina and her family. They lived in Pittsburg. Aunt Nicolina was his mother's sister. Andrew, who every one called Andy, was tired of going to Pittsburg. He considered going to Hawaii. He hesitated going anywhere alone because of the experience he had a couple of years ago. He hated going anywhere alone.

Andy then went back to thinking of how he had gotten to where he is now. Andy had graduated as an Electronic Engineer. He had gone to work for an Aerospace company. He worked two years and was tired of the work they gave him. most of the assignments Andy was given were writing proposals or manuals. When he did get a chance at engineering work he was assigned making test equipment at an Arizona plant. one weekend while in Arizona, he decided to visit the grand Canyon. He remembered that he didn't enjoy it. He had only looked down once and then returned to his motel. It was no fun unless he could share what he saw with someone. He remembers not liking any of the jobs they gave him, so at the beginning of the school year he had decided to go to night school to get his master's Degree. He felt that if he had a higher degree he would be given better assignments. one evening Andy was eating in the school cafeteria and he was explaining to a friend, who was a mechanical engineering student, what electricity was. He was explaining it in terms of comparing the flow of electricity with water flowing through a hose. The Dean of the Engineering Department happened to hear him and was impressed. He offered Andy a job teaching Electronics in the Evening Division. Andy had accepted and taught one semester. He found that he loved teaching. The next semester the Dean of Engineering had asked Andy what his salary was at the Aerospace Company. The Dean offered Andy a day time job at a greater salary than he was getting at the Aerospace Company. Andy remembered that it was that job that brought Andy where he is now. That was why he hesitated to travel. Would he enjoy it if he couldn't share it with anyone?

After much consideration, Andy decided to go to Hawaii. He made travel arrangements and reservations at the outrigger Hotel. The travel took most of the day. When he got to the hotel he ate Dinner and went to bed early. The next day he went to breakfast and toured the city and the grounds around the hotel. After lunch he decided to go swimming on the beach. The city tour had almost made him decide that he was through seeing any more of Hawaii. Perhaps it was just him that had the problem. But he didn't enjoy sightseeing if he couldn't share it with someone. He walked out on the beach laid his towel on an empty chair under one of the umbrellas and went into the water. He had not noticed that there was a towel on the other chair under the umbrella. He swam down the shore line not wanting to go too far from the shore. After swimming for several minutes he tired and headed back to shore and the chair under the umbrella. He didn't want to get too much sun. After siting he noticed the towel on the other chair. While he was wondering whose it was a young woman came, picked up the towel and sat down.

"I'm sorry," said Andy. "Am I taking some ones place on this chair?"

"Not that I know of," she replied. "You don't need this other chair do you?"

"No," answered Andy. "I'm here by myself."

"Isn't it kind of lonely coming here by yourself," asked the woman?

How about you, are you here alone also," asked Andy. "Are you waiting for someone? I can give up the chair if you need it."

"No, I'm not here with anyone,"said the woman."I was supposed to be here with my fiancé, but at the last minute he had to go on a business trip."

"Then if you are here alone, why did you ask me if it was kind of lonely for me here alone? You have done the same thing." The woman started to laugh,

"I thought I was going to have company," said the woman laughing. It does sound funny doesn't it? By the way, my name is Christina Corelli. most of my friends call me Tina.

"Hi Tina," said Andy. "It's nice to meet you. my name is Andrew Brown. All my friends call me Andy."

"Nice to meet you too," said Tina. "It is lonely being here alone. It's also kind of embarrassing."

"I know," said Andy, especially when you look around at all the other umbrellas and see all the couples. Look at that one over there. The two are kissing.

"I never thought it would be like this," said Tina.

"Corelli, that is an Italian name," said Andy. "my mother is Italian. my father is Swedish.

"My fiancé, Paul, is german so I will have a german name. "You weren't going to share a room with Paul were you?" Asked Andy?

"No of course not," said Tina looking disappointed at his question. "I'm sorry," said Andy. "There are so many couples now that sleep together and get married sometimes later, if at all."

"Well not me," explained Tina. "I would never do that. I am a Born Again Christian."

"You're kidding," said Andy with a surprised look on his face. "I am a Born Again Christian too."

"That is great," said Tina. "It is nice to meet another true Christian." They sat awhile not saying anything. Then Andy broke the silence.

"Tell me about your fiancé," asked Andy.

"He` is a very intelligent man," started Tina "He is an industrial attorney. He is very classy. He is always well dressed. He is a good catch. How about you, what do you for a living?"

"I graduated as an Electronic Engineer. I worked two years and was unhappy at what I was doing. Then the Dean of Engineering at a local college offered me a job. So now I am a college instructor." "That is great," said Tina. "We have that in common. I am a high school science teacher." They both smiled. After a few minutes of silence Andy reopened the conversation.

"If you are a Born Again Christian that brings up a question," said Andy. "Aren't all Italians Catholic?"

"We used to be but we changed. It's a long story. I don't think you want to hear it."

"I would love to hear it. But why don't you give me the short version."

"Well alright," said Tina. "I hope I don't bore you. my uncle and aunt live next door to my parents. They used to go to church with my parents. one day they didn't show up to go to church with them. When they were approached they told my parents that they had changed church. When asked why they gave my parents a Bible and told them to study it. my father did and he found so many places where the Catholic Church has varied from the Bible. my dad then visited several churches and found that everything that the Baptist Church did was completely centered on the Bible."

"That is amazing," said Andy. "There aren't too many of us these days."

While she was talking her phone rang. Andy could tell by the way she talked that it was her fiancé. However, when she finished her conversation her expression turned to sadness.

"I don't know what to do," she said after putting her phone away. "That was my fiancé. He is not coming at all. He has a new client to win over."

"He can't make it at all in two weeks," said Andy. "Does he care more for his business then you?"

"Apparently," said Tina. "I don't know what to do. I am thinking like you. I don't think I would enjoy being here alone. I probably should go home."

"I have a suggestion that may solve both our problems," said Andy. "I am with you on one thing. I have considered just staying here or going home. I don't like being alone out here. I originally came to see all the wonderful things that there is to see here in Hawaii. So here is my suggestion. I am a Born Again Christian and you have nothing to fear from me. I also accept that you have a fiancé who you care for very much. So why don't we as friends be partners on this vacation. We can stay here and act like a couple if that would make you feel less embarrassed. Also if you want we can travel all over the islands of Hawaii and enjoy it together." Tina looked at Andy for a while and then smiling she asked.

"Do you mean we would spend the two weeks as pretend boyfriend and girlfriend?"

"If that is what you want to call it," said Andy. "I have one condition. It will be like dating a good friend. I have never let any of my dates pay their own way. I don't want to ever break that record. It would make me feel bad."

"Wow," said Tina. "You are something else." "Does that mean yes," asked Andy?

"What do you have in mind," asked Tina?

"Well first," started Andy, "we will spend a couple of days swimming here, eating together to let people think we are a couple. This will give me time to plan where we will go, and what we want to see. I can also make reservations for hotels, transportation, on the other islands we want to visit."

"Will you show me what you come up with before you make reservations," asked Tina?

"Of course," said Andy. "We are in this together."

The next two days they stayed at the outrigger Hotel. They ate breakfast and lunch together. After lunch they went out to the beach to swim to get to know each other better. They spent time in the water playing like two little kids. He would dive under grab her feet and push her up out of the water. She would splash water into his face then as she would swim away she would go under water and grab his feet and do the same thing to him. They really enjoyed those two days and really got to know each other. However Andy started to worry. He thought she was beautiful the first time he met her. But now he began to see what an upbeat and sweet person she was. He told himself to be careful and not fall in love with her. After all, she was engaged to a very classy man as she had mentioned several times.

"I wonder," said Tina "I came here by cab. Do you have a car"? "Yes,' answered Andy. "I rented a car as soon as I landed here.

Remember I had planned on seeing all of Hawaii alone."

The next day they met for breakfast. After eating, Andy laid down a sheet with information he had written that night before he went to bed.

"Listen, Tina," he started. "It was not possible to set up an agenda for the next few days in traveling through Hawaii. First of all we have no idea on how long we will stay at any place. We may want to stay at one of the other islands for two or three days. So let's play it by ear day by day."

"Look Andy," said Tina. "I'm sorry. I should not have asked to see an agenda. I trust you. You are the leader. Take me were ever you decide to go.

"All right then," said Andy. "Let's eat lunch early and be ready to go to our first sightseeing tour."

"Great," said Tina. "I will be ready. Shall we eat about eleven thirty?"

"That will be perfect," responded Andy.

After they ate lunch they got into Andy's car and started on their way. Andy found route 90 and proceeded west.

"I think the first place we should go is to Pearl Harbor and see the Arizona monument," informed Andy.

"You're the guide," said Tina. After driving for a while they came to a large sign that read, USS Arizona memorial. Andy parked the car and they walked to the sign.

"It would be nice to have a picture of us in front of the sign," said Tina? There was another couple that was standing there admiring the area. Andy turned to them.

"Sir," said Andy to the fellow. "Would you mind taking a picture of me and my girlfriend in front of the sign?"

"I'd be happy to," said the fellow." And while we are at it would you take a picture of me and my wife?"

"I'd love to," said Andy. "Take two pictures if you will, just in case one doesn't come out good. If you like I will take two of you." They agreed. Andy put his arms around Tina and wondered if Tina would object. She didn't so for the second shot he squeezed her tightly. She didn't object. Andy wondered if she would ever show that picture to her fiancé. After that they walked down the path down toward the water. At the water's edge there was a small building that was named visitor Center.

"Let's go see what is inside," suggested Andy.

"OK," said Tina. They walked inside. In the middle of the room was a large model of the Arizona. It sat on a bench that was about ten feet long. They could see small details of the ship. Andy and Tina studied it for a few minutes and then walked around the room look-ing at other naval objects that were displayed. After they were satisfied, they walked out onto the pier. They looked out and saw a small boat traveling toward a long narrow building on an island in the middle of the harbor. There was another boat on the pier that was loading people on it. Andy and Tina got on also. The boat had seats like a bus except it was much wider. As they got closer, they had a better view of the building they were going to. It was long and narrow. There were large openings on each side like glassless windows. They landed on a small landing port that extended out of the building. Andy and Tina got off and followed the others down the building. They all walked looking out of the right side openings that had small fences to protect the visitors.

"I can see things down in the water," said Tina, "but I can't make out what they are."

"They are things that are on the decks of the Arizona," said Andy, "They could be gun turrets." As they continued down the building they came to a place where an object was sticking out of the water.

"What is that," asked Tina?

"It could be a smoke stack," said Andy. Although it is much larger then I would expect it to be." As they walked down towards the other end they saw small parts sticking out of the water but they couldn't tell what they were. They walked down to the other end of the building, where there was a large sign that covered most of the wall. It was a memorial of all the gallant men that were entombed there. Andy felt a small chill reading the sign. They soon left the area feeling excited at what they were visiting. As the boat was taking them back to the pier, Andy looked out of the side of the boat.

"Tina, look at the other side of the lake," said Andy. "What do you see?"

"I see another boat," said Tina.

"I think it is a World War 11 submarine," said Andy. "I think we should go there next." They left the area feeling they had visited history.

They next traveled down route 90 till they got to the sign that read, US Navy Pier. They walked into the grounds toward a larger sign that read Bowfin Park. Just before they got to the sign, at the cement entrance way, they saw on the ground two objects one on each side of the sign.

"What are these," asked Tina? "They look like torpedoes."

"I think they are torpedoes," said Andy. "These are the symbols that tell us that we are at the entrance to the submarine."

Again they asked another tourist to take their picture. This time they did it with both Andy's camera and Tina's camera. She wanted her own record of their trips. They walked past the sign down the path to the water where they saw the submarine. People were coming off the sub and a few were waiting for their turn to go into the sub.

"We had better get into line before that group behind us gets here," stated Andy.

"Do we really want to go inside," asked Tina. "There is a building over there. It probably has a model just like the other building had a model of the Arizona."

"I think we should go in," said Andy. "If for no other reason except to be able to tell your children and grandchildren that you were in a submarine."

"All right," said Tina. "You have a good point." They got in line and didn't have wait too long before they were allowed to enter the sub. They walked across the deck to the entrance and climbed down the ladder to the interior of the sub.

"Wow," said Tina. "It is very narrow in here. What are these holes in end of the sub?"

"Those are the torpedo tubes. There are four here and I think there are four at the other end of the sub. As they went into the next compartment Andy was able to point out a small area as the radio room. The next thing they walked by was the sleeping area. There were two bunk beds on each side of the narrow passage way. As they continued down the compartment they came to the kitchen.

"That is the smallest kitchen I ever saw," said Tina. As they got to the main area Andy explained the periscope that was down with the handles on the floor.

There were a few areas that had so many gadgets, instruments and meters that Andy couldn't explain. When they went back to the surface they toured around the deck.

"See these round tube like things on the side of the sub," said Andy. "They are the ships ballast tanks. They fill them with water when they want to submerge."

"Very interesting," said Tina. "You know, Andy, I'm glad you talked me into going into the sub." After leaving the sub they went into the little building next to the dock. There they saw a large model of the sub. one side of the sub was open so that you could see all that was inside. Tina enjoyed studying the model, remembering every area they had actually been in.

Finally they left the area and got back on route 90. From there Andy checking his map transferred to route 92. They drove for about a half hour when Tina, looking out of the window, broke the silence. "Look at all the strange plants," she said. "They go on for miles.

I don't recognize them. I wonder what they are."

"I think they are pineapples," said Andy. "There are a lot of pineapple farms here." He had barely finished speaking when they came up to a sign which said 'Dole Plantation'. They pulled up to the building and went into the visitor's entrance. After looking at all the displays, they went outside and had pictures taken in front of the main building which had the sign in front. From there they continued down high way 90 for a little over a half hour and transfer to route 83. Not long after that they came up to a sign that read Waimea valley. They parked the car and entered the visitor's Center. There they got a pamphlet that showed them everything there was to see. They proceeded down the path. The pamphlet said that the Botanical gardens could be seen at various locations throughout the park. As they proceeded down the path they saw so many wild animals, like goats and a variety of birds. It took them over an hour to get to the other end. on the way they both enjoyed the trip. At the other end they came to a high waterfall. It was about two hundred feet or more high, Andy guessed. It was only about ten feet wide. They found two empty seats in front of the lake where many other visitors were seated. Andy and Tina sat down and to watch whatever was going on.

"That is so beautiful," said Tina with a wondering look on her face. "I can never thank you for taking me here." Then, "Look," she said with an excited sound to her voice. "There are two men about three quarter of the way up on the side of the cliff. Don't they worry about falling?"

"I think they are part of the act," said Andy. "Look higher; there is another one on top of the cliff. I would suggest that you hold your breath." It was about five minutes later that one of the man took a frightening dive into the lake below. The other one started climbing higher to meet the other man who was already on top of the cliff.

"What are they going to do," asked Tina? "They aren't going to dive from up there are they?"

"This is their show," said Andy. "I'm sure they have some type of an act to perform." The two men stood there for a while and finally they both raised their hands up in the air and jumped. on the way down they made a flip and landed beautifully with their hand over their heads.

"I'm impressed," said Tina.

"Now look on the other side of the falls," suggested Andy. There is a fellow climbing up that cliff. It is about a hundred feet higher than the falls." As he got near the top suddenly he slipped and dropped about two feet. The audience moaned, but he caught himself on a rock and continued climbing up the cliff.

"I wonder if that was all part of the act," said Andy.

"It worked," said Tina." When the man got to the top of the hill he stood at the edge of the cliff and raised his hand for a while. Every one stood in awe wondering what he was about to do. Suddenly he took a leap out as far as he could and dived into the water. Every one clapped. The three men sat at the end of the lake and rested.

"I think the show is over," said Andy. He was right. Everyone seated there got up and started to leave. "I think the divers are resting getting ready for the next show. I think we had better leave. It is getting late. I would like to see more of the park." They left and walked down the path towards the entrance. They stopped at the sign that said, Bauhinia. They watch the hula dancers. From there they visited the Kauhale (Hawaiian Living Site) where they saw the grass huts and the Hawaiian rowboats. From there they approached the entrance.

"I feel kind of hungry," said Tina. "It is almost seven thirty." "Where did the time go," said Andy. "I am very hungry. Let's stop at 'The Proud Peacock Restaurant.' It is here at the entrance." They found it and had dinner. After dinner, as they walked out, Tina commented.

"I don't know what it was that we ate," said Tina, "but it was delicious." They both laughed. At the entrance they found a gift store called 'Waimea valley Store. Andy bought a Tee-shirt with a picture of the falls and the name of the park. Tina bought a Hawaiian souvenir jewelry. They got back to the hotel after nine so, being tired, they went directly to bed.

The next morning, they ate breakfast early.

"I think I would like to see more of this island before we move on to another island.

"We have plans to see other islands," said Tina?

"Of course," said Andy, "that is where most of the fantastic things to see are. I want to see the grand Canyon of the Pacific on Kauai and the volcanoes on the Big Island."

"Sounds fascinating," said Tina. "When do we start?" They left about ten and Andy drove east around Diamond Head down route 72 to route 83 down the east shore. It was a very scenic route. They stopped at Waiahole Beach Park. It was the along the shore drive. It was beautiful. They walked around the grassy knoll. on the way they stopped at five more beach Parks. They were all very scenic. At about lunch time they arrived at the Polynesian Cultural Center. It was the most impressive entrance they had ever seen. The sign was about 100 feet wide. The sign was cream colored and had gold colored letters. It said 'Polynesian Cultural Center' across the complete sign. Inside Andy and Tina were delighted at all the Hawaiian music and hula dancing they watched. As they roamed through the Center they stopped at several outdoor shows. They spent most of the day circulating from one grass shack to another greatly enjoying the Hawaiian displays. At one shack, where the one side was completely open, they noticed there were several seats inside. Some people were already siting there waiting for the performers. Andy and Tina entered and sat down waiting with others. About ten minutes later a young woman came in with a drum that was shaped like a large ball attached to a smaller ball. It was a Hawaii drum. A dancer then came in and the girl with the drum beat a rhythm on the drum and sang while the dancer danced. It was fantastic. They were so talented. Next they followed the crowd to the river. They sat at the edge of the river and watched the floats go by. Each float had a different show on it. most of them were different dancers with different costumes. There must have been twenty or more floats. on route they heard that the evening show at the Pacific Pavilion near the entrance way, started at seven thirty. Andy and Tina decided they wanted to see the show. So at about six thirty they went to the gateway Restaurant to eat dinner. After dinner they were just in time to see the show. The show was great. First there were about twenty five female dancers who wore all white dresses. They danced in perfect unison. They danced several different dances. Next came about the same amount of men. They were dressed in some kind of Hawaiian uniforms. Their dances were different than the women's dances. Their dances were more like warrior dances. The last performer was the fire juggler. He juggled several fire stick with great speed. He did different dances each more dangerous than the one before.

"I wonder how many scars he has from mistakes he made in the past," said Tina. Andy laughed at her statement. The show lasted until nine thirty. on the way to the hotel Andy turned to Tina.

"Let's get up early tomorrow," said Andy. "We have a plane to catch to go to Kauai. Pack one of your smaller suitcases for about a four to five days trip. Pick one of the smaller ones of the six that you brought."

"Ha-ha," said Tina. "You are very funny. I only brought three suitcases."

"I was close," said Andy. "I only brought two. one big one and a smaller one that I knew I would need to travel to the other islands." "I had the same forethought," said Tina. "I have one that will be perfect." Through the entire conversation nether one stopped laughing. When they got to the hotel, being very tired, they went straight to bed.

The next morning they got up early, had a quick breakfast and drove to the airport.

"Where are we going to stay at when we get there," asked Tina. "I checked with the outrigger clerk. She told me that the outrigger has a hotel in Kauai. I made reservations for two rooms." After a short flight, they arrived at the Lihue Airport at about ten. They drove to the hotel to check in and drop off their suitcases.

Andy made a few phone calls from his room.

"I called for helicopter reservations," said Andy when he met Tina for breakfast. "They are booked up for today. I made reservation for tomorrow at eight o'clock. They recommended that we spend time at the Waimea Canyon Lookout. I think first, I would like to see the Fern grotto."

That's fine with me," said Tina. After getting instructions from the hotel clerk on how to get to the Fern grotto, they drove north on route 56 to the city of Wailua. From there they drove to the Wailua River State Park. There they got on the open-air boat call Smiths. There were several people who apparently were going to the same place. The ship headed west along the river. The boat trip itself was very interesting. The Wailua River winded through dense tropical growth. There were hills all around the river. About every hundred feet or so there was small water fall. Andy looked at Tina. Her face had that wondering look like she was seeing something she had not expected. Andy loved her very sweet and beautiful face. Soon they arrived at their destination. Everyone got out and started to walk down a very narrow path. Everyone was amazed at the different plants that lined the pathway. There were flowers on both sides that they had never seen before. The trip down the path alone was worth the trip. Finally they got to the grotto. It was a lava rock grotto. It was about five feet above the ground. There was a path on the left side that led up to the hollow cave like opening. There was a metal fence on the outside of the area to keep visitors from falling. The front of the area was fringed with hanging ferns. Andy, Tina, and two other couples climbed up and stood by the fence. most stood there to have their picture taken. Andy and Tina also took pictures. A friendly fellow took pictures of Andy and Tina together. This gave Andy a chance to hug Tina tightly. He loved the feel of her body against his. Her body was so soft. Suddenly a young Hawaiian appeared with a mandolin and started to play Hawaiian music. Andy and Tina loved it so much they stayed longer then they had expected. Final they returned to the dock to wait for the boat. When it came they climbed aboard and were surprised that there was a beautiful young Hawaiian hula dance that danced in the aisle all the way back to the park entrance. Tina could not stop talking about how much fun she had.

"I think we should spend the rest of the day at the Waimea Canyon Lookout," said Andy. "If this map is correct the Spouting Horn is on the way."

"Sounds like a good plan to me," said Tina. "I want to compliment you. You have done a fantastic job so far. I have complete trust in you."

"Why thank you so much," said Andy. "That is so sweet." "By the way," asked Tina, "what is a Spouting Horn?"

I'm not sure," answered Andy. "It may be some sort of a falls." Andy then headed south on route on route 50. Since the hotel was on the way they stopped and had lunch.

"You know," said Andy. "About half of our vacation is over and we have a lot to see yet."

"So what if we go over," said Tina. "School doesn't start for a couple of months."

"Don't you think Paul would be worried," said Andy trying to find out if she was thinking of him.

"He had his chance," said Tina. "He would have hated this trip anyway. He is a city boy." After lunch Andy headed south until he got to route 520. He then turned down route 520 following the sign that directed them to Spouting Horn. When he got to the waterfront he parked his car and they walked to the shore. There was no beach. The waterfront was all covered with large rocks. There were several people standing there with them. Andy was about to ask them what was going on when they hear this loud hissing sound. Suddenly, a large blast of water come sprouting up out from between the rocks. It was about half way between the water and the highway. They were shocked at first then they stood there waiting for the next sprout.

"Look down the road," said Tina. "There are smaller water spout, but they accrue more often. What caused this?" she asked walking down where the small water spouts were accruing. Andy followed her.

"If you watch the ocean water, notice that the spouts occur when the waves come in. I think that as the waves come in they caused a pressure under the rock and that causes the water to spout out where it can find a hole."

"Yes, I can see that," said Tina. "It makes perfect sense." They stayed there enjoying the spouts and the sound it made. After a while they decided to take a walk around the park across the road. It was so beautiful with small trees some pretty flowers and a trimmed lawn to walk on. Finally they left. Andy took route 520 back to route 50 and he headed west. He drove for almost an hour before he got to the sign that directed him to Waimea Canyon Drive. on the way they passed an airfield.

"That is where we will be coming tomorrow to get our helicopter ride," said Andy. "It is a little less than an hour to get here. So we had better leave about seven am."

"I'll be ready," said Tina. Andy took route 550A north. The sign said that it was the Waimea Canyon Drive. There were several lookout points along the way but Andy was looking for the Waimea Canyon Lookout. Soon the road changed to 55B. A short drive later they reach the lookout he wanted. They parked and walked down the path along the side of the mountain. Tina walked to the edge and looked down at the land below.

"This is fantastic," she said with a sweet voice. "This is a stunning view of the valleys and tropical forests below. I am amazed at the different colors of the land. Andy, look down there. It is not only the beautiful green color of the forest but the variation of the ground. Look the hill is a reddish brown. The other side of it is light brown."

"It is beautiful," said Andy. "I see what you mean. There is a stunning variation in color." Andy then pulled out the pamphlet he had about the lookout. "It says here that the grand Canyon Lookout provides idyllic scenery of the Kauai's lush valleys and tropical forests."

"That is an understatement," said Tina. "Let's follow the hiking trail that takes us around this mountain. There must be a lot of more amazing scenery to see."

"The pamphlet says that the hiking trail is forty miles long and is 3600 feet high," said Andy with a kidding smile on his face.

"Do you have other plans for today," said Tina kidding back. "Let's go a little way and see how it goes." It went very well. They walked down the trail for over an hour. Tina was right. At every turn they saw something different. Finally they turned back. After leaving the area Andy took route 50 back to Lihue where he changed to route 56 and headed north.

"What have you got to mind now," asked Tina.

"It is still early," said Andy. "Let's see what is on the west and north coast of this island. The map show that the road goes mostly along the coast. on the way up the coast they stopped at several beaches. They were all different and very scenic. They drove and stopped at Kilauea Point. There they found the Charo's Restaurant. It was a fabulous place. After taking pictures out front they went in and had a delicious dinner. They got back to the hotel late so they went right to bed. After all they had to get up early the next morning.

The next morning they got to the airport at seven forty five. They were soon in the air. There was music in the aircraft while they were flying. They soon left the flat area and went in to the canyon. Andy had been to the grand Canyon in Utah. This was more exciting. The sides of the grand Canyon in the US were sloping. It had a trail down the sides to the river at the bottom. This canyon had sides that went straight down. As they flew down inside the canyon Andy noticed something on the other side.

"Look Tina," said Andy, "do you see something close to the other side of the canyon?"

"I don't see anything," she answered. "Look closely," suggested Andy.

"All I see is something that looks like a bird," said Tina.

"That is not a bird," said Andy. "That is another helicopter that is returning to the airport. That should tell you something about the width of the canyon."

"It must be miles wide," said Tina with a surprised tone.

"I think that it is much larger then it seems when you have nothing to compare it with," said Andy. "By the way, did you know that the nick name for this canyon is, The grand Canyon of the Pacific?" As they left the deep part of the canyon they flew over the hills and valleys that they had seen a small part of on their lookout trip.

"My goodness, Andy," said Tina. "This is fantastic. Look at all the colors of red, orange, blended with the different shades of brown that covers the land. Andy, this artistry creation can only be painted by the hand of god."

"Boy, now you are becoming poetic," said Andy. Tina only smiled at him. They both enjoyed the trip and felt sorry when it was over. When they were back in the car driving back to the hotel Tina turned to Andy.

"That was fantastic. It gets better all the time. Where do we go from here?"

"We go to the hotel repack for the next three or four days and go to the airport. We are going to the island that is referred as the Big Island.

After they packed their suitcases they drove to the airport. The next flight to the Big Island was at four. They arrived at the Kona International Airport at about five. They drove to the Waikoloa hotel and checked it. It was too late to travel so they settled in the hotel for the evening. The hotel was very luxurious. It had a beautiful swimming pool in the rear of the hotel. Andy and Tina ate dinner at about six and spent the rest of the evening wandering around the hotel enjoying the beautiful grounds.

The next morning they ate breakfast at the hotel enjoying the atmosphere around the hotel. At about ten they decided to travel to the Hawai'i volcanoes National Park. The park was on the other side of the island. Andy felt that this trip may take them all day. Andy took route 190 to route 19. on the way they stopped and enjoyed visiting the Akaka Falls and the Hawai'i Tropical Botanical garden. At the city of Hilo they took route 11. This road led to the volcanoes National Park. The road down route 11 was mostly uphill. After going through some harden lava the came to an area that was green with shrubs, tropical trees and flowers.

"That is fantastic," said Tina. "We went from a lava covered area to a beautiful tropical garden." They went down the road for about ten minutes and they came to a sign that read, mountain view. Andy pulled off the road and they walked to the edge the cliff. "We have plenty of time so let's see all that we can see," suggested Andy. Tina agreed. So they walked around the area and enjoyed the scenery. Fifteen minutes later they got into the car and proceeded down the road. About twenty minutes later they came to Akatsuka orchard gardens. They walked through the gardens. It was very hilly so they walked up and down hills paths and steep steps. Andy took every opportunity to hold her hand in the excuse of keep her from falling. They had a very enjoyable time. Soon they got back on the road. The road now took them up the mountain. All the areas on both sides were covered with lava rock. When they got to the Hawai'i volcanoes National Park they got off route 11 and headed on a road going into the park. They felt like they were in the middle of a lava flow. When they got near the top of the mountain they saw that the road was blocked. Lava had flowed across it at one time and hardened. Andy pulled up to the side of the road and parked behind a car that had already parked there. He saw people walking down the road on top of the lava. They were headed toward the right towards the ocean.

"Let's see what they are going to see," said Andy. "It looks safe. If you noticed they are walking toward the ocean. In front of them is a cloud. I think it is steam from the lava flowing into the ocean."

"Do you think it is safe," asked Tina?

"Those people think it is," said Andy. "Don't worry. I will be right beside you." He took her hand and they walked up on the lava and proceeded towards a sign that was about fifty feet down from the edge of the lava. When they got to the sign they read it. It said;

Danger Hazardous Fumes Steep Cliffs Rough Surface Hot Lava

"Let's go in and when it looks bad we will return," said Tina, in effect notifying Andy that she was willing to try.

"I think I would like a picture in front of this sign first," said Andy, He then asked the older couple that were standing next to the sign if they would take their picture. They agreed and took their picture.

"Hi," said Tina. "You are staying at the Waikoloa hotel as we are.

We have seen you there."

"Yes," responded the woman. "We also saw you at the airport. We were in line with you to rent a car."

"I also think that we sat in the table next to you for breakfast this morning," added Tina. "my name is Tina and this is Andy."

"Nice to meet you," said the woman. my name is Nancy Karen and this is my husband Fred." They shook hands. Suddenly a young man came running up to them.

"Mom and Dad," he yelled. "We have to leave right now. They have moved up the meeting two days. I have to be at Hilo at six."

"It is now only three," said Andy. "You have three hours to get there."

"I have to take my parents back to the hotel, responded the young man. That is on the other side of the island. It would take about an hour and a half and then I would have to come back here."

"Can't your parent go with you," asked Tina.

"My meeting is going to be in a hotel conference room. I have no idea how long it will last. They were talking about going to dinner if we can't come to an agreement. I will probably be there all night."

"This is our son David," said Nancy. "The reason we are here is because of his meeting."

"I have an idea," said Tina turning to Andy to get his support. "Why don't the Karens come with us?

"That is a good Idea," said Andy. "We are going back to the hotel. However we are going back the southern and western road. We may want to stop a few places on the way back but what else are you going to do sitting at the hotel."

"Oh that is so nice of you," said Nancy. "But we hate to burden you."

"Nonsense," said Tina. "We would like the company."

"If you are sure we wouldn't be a burden on you," said Fred. "We would love to go with you."

"It's all settled then," said Andy.

"Great," said David. "Now we all can see the lava flow. David then put his arm around his mother and they started up the lava rock towards the ocean.

Andy and Tina also started walking towards the ocean. As they walked they could see streaks of red hot lava flowing in between cracks in the lava rocks. They could feel the heat on their feet. The lava rocks were hot. They made sure they walked on the higher lava rocks that were cooler and farther from the hot flowing lava. They did make it to the edge of the cliff. They could see the hot red lava pouring out from under the lava rock into the ocean. The hot lava caused the water to vaporize, causing a great cloud. going back was as tricky as going there.

"I'm so glad we came here and walked on the hot lava rock," said Tina. "It will be something to tell my kids and grandkids. This is something I could never forget." Fred and Nancy were already standing near Andy's car. David had already left for his meeting.

"Well let's get into the car and go for a ride," said Andy. Fred and Nancy got into the back seat. Tina rode in front with Andy. Andy then got back on route 11 and headed south. They spent a few minutes at the Punalu'u Beach Park and the Whittington Beach Park. They drove around the south shore point and headed north on the west coast of the island. They spent several minutes at ocean view. They were very high at this point and the view looking down at the ocean was fantastic. They headed north stopping at a few parks but soon got tired of the parks and they headed to the hotel. They got there at about six. It was time for dinner. As they walked into the lobby they saw a sigh that said a luau was taking place at six thirty.

"Let's go to the luau," suggested Andy. "I have never been to one" "That is a great idea," said Tina. "I would like to say that I have been to one. Nancy and Fred, would you like to join us?"

"I think that would be fun," said Nancy. "We would love to join you." With that they proceeded to the luau. As they walked in they could see two men digging the area where they had cooked the pig.

"Do they cook the pig underground," asked Tina?

"I think they wrap it in something and then build a fire over it," said Andy. They each got a drink, found a table for the four of them and they sat down. In front of the men digging was a long narrow table. A few women were bringing large pans of different foods to go with the meat.

"What is that platform on the other side opposite the serving table," asked Fred?

"I think that it is a performing platform," said Andy. "I hope they will be performing for us later."

Have you guys just arrived in Hawai'i," asked Tina of Nancy. "No," answered Nancy. "We have been to all the islands. This is our last stop. my son is an Industrial Attorney. He travels all over the world for his company. They help corporations buy other corporations. He asked us to go with him on vacation. Since he wasn't sure how long his meeting was going take, could take several days, we decided to come two week before his meeting. How about you guys, what islands have you visited?"

"We landed first on oahu," said Andy. "Then we went to Kauai and then to here, the Big Island. Next we are going to maui and then back to oahu."

"You have not been to maui," said Nancy? "We just came from there. You have to go and stay at The Palms at Wailea. It is the most wonderful place in Hawaii. It is like a peaceful haven. We stayed there an extra day because it was restful and relaxing.

"We will be going tomorrow," said Andy. Thank you for the information." The food was not ready till seven. When the signal was given that the food was ready, the people all formed a line to get the food. The four of them got into the line and filled their plates with food. They were just starting to eat when they heard music coming from the platform across the area. Soon Hawaiian dancers started to perform. There were four different groups that danced different dances. Two groups were male and two groups were female. They were very entertaining. Andy and his group got seconds while the food was still available. It was past eleven when the Fire Dancers come on. There were four of them. They each had two sticks that were on fire. They danced and twirled the staffs so fast that it was hard to follow their movements. At midnight everything started to close down. Andy, Tina and the Karens left together. When they got to the hotel lobby, they turned toward each other to say goodbye.

"It was so nice to meet you," said Nancy. "You are a very sweet couple. I hope you will both be very happy."

"We are so happy to meet you," said Tina. "You have been such wonderful company. Wish you could come with us to maui."

"That would be such fun. But we have to get back." She then turned and saying good bye she hugged Andy. Tina felt the same so she saying goodbye hugged Fred. They parted with sorrow in their hearts.

The next morning they got up late. They were tired since they went to bed late. They ate breakfast and headed for the airport. They got the next available flight to maui. They landed at maui's Kahului Airport at about one ten. They rented a car and drove down route 31 to Wailea. Andy drove around until he found the Palms Resort. It was all that Nancy had said. It had stone walls on each side of the entrance way. Inside was like a small village. There must be about one hundred condos. They saw a souvenir store and a restaurant.

They checked in and were fortunate to find one at the edge of the ocean. They drove to the condo and entered it.

"Is this alright with you," asked Andy?

"I don't know," said Tina. "I thought that it was going to be like two apartments." Are we going to stay in the same apartment?"

"It is like two hotel rooms," said Andy. "We just have a common bathroom. Besides, I don't think you want a whole condo by yourself." They started to look around the condo. It had two very large beautiful bed-rooms on the far side of the building. The main room was a large room with a small kitchen at the entrance side. The opposite side went out onto a porch. The whole condo was on ground level. They went out on the back porch. on the left, was a small hill, which was covered with lava rocks. Andy looked at his map. The map called it the Lava Beds. There were no condos on that side. on the right was a small stream that went down to the ocean. It was about a foot deep all the way with several one foot water falls all the way down to the ocean. on both sides were tropical plants that acted like fences. on the other side of the stream there were condos as far as you could see. "I think it will be alright," said Tina. "I trust you. Besides, it is so beautiful."

"Ok then," said Andy. "Let's go get some lunch and go out and see some of the sights. Tomorrow we will go up the Haleakala National Park and look down at the craters from the mountain top." They went to the restaurant and had lunch. It was two forty five when they left the condo. Andy got back on route 31 and took it north. Andy decided to stop at Kalama Park. out on the ocean they watched several surfers riding the waves.

"That looks like fun," said Tina. "You want to try it," asked Andy?" "You are so funny," responded Tina. "You know Andy, we have been to several parks and beaches and somehow we never get tired of seeing them. They are all different." After spending about an hour enjoying the different plants in the park, they left and headed north. on the way they saw a truck parked on the side of the road with two other cars pulled behind it. The sign said Fresh Pineapples served here.

"What do you say Tina," said Andy. "Would you like a fresh pineapple?"

"Can we eat it here," asked Tina?"

"Can't you see those people eating one, said Andy? The woman who is selling them cuts the top off and with a long knife chop it up inside its shell. He then gives it to the buyer with a plastic spoon."

"I'm game," said Tina. Andy ordered two and they ate them while standing by the car.

"Well what do you think?" asked Andy after they finished.

"I can't believe how delicious that was," said Tina. "They must have just picked it off the vine." They then got into the car and headed north. When Andy got to route 310 he took it to route 30. After a while on route 30 they came to maui Tropical Plantation. There they saw several waterfalls. Some were several hundred feet high. They saw about six altogether. At the far end they saw tropical plants they had not seen before.

"I would never have believed that there were that many different plants and flowers," stated Tina.

"You understand most of that is that most of these plans will not grow any place else," said Andy. Next they headed north on 30 till they got to Iao valley State Park. It was the most fantastic they had seen to date. The mountains were very tall but narrow coming to a point at the top. It was not just one. There were dozens surrounding them. Andy looked at Tina. The look of wonderment showed clearly on her face.

"How did these, I don't know what to call them, come out of the ground," asked Tina? "I find it hard to call them mountains."

"The sign here calls them Kukaemoku," said Andy. "However my map calls them Iao Needles. The best that I could describe them is that they look like giant unopened umbrellas."They walked around the whole park taking in the wonders of the area. They found it was hard to leave.

"I think we had better head for home," said Andy. "It is getting close to five thirty. That said, they headed for the condo. They got there a little after six. one at a time they went into the bathroom to clean up and about six thirty they went out for dinner. After dinner Andy bought some nuts and chips and they sat on the porch and watch the sun go down.

The next morning they ate breakfast early and left to go on their next sightseeing adventure.

"Why do you want to leave so early," asked Tina.

"I want to leave early because the Haleakala National Park that I would like to take us to is on the other side of the island. Because of the rough mountain terrain there are no roads going directly there. Besides I would like to come back early so that we can enjoy the condo this afternoon and maybe go swimming in the ocean.

"Sounds great to me," said Tina. "You have not let me down yet. In fact I don't know how I will ever thank you."

"No thanks are necessary," said Andy. "I am enjoying it as much as you do. In fact it is I that should thank you. You have been a wonderful companion." Andy took route 31 north until he got to mokulele Highway. A half hour later they passed the airport and got on route 37. The sign said it was Haleakala Highway. Andy then headed south. Just after they got to the city of Pukalani the highway got narrow and very slow driving. Twenty minutes later they got to Haleakala Crater road. It was worse than the previous road. It twisted around hills and mountains. There was a small space were the road was pretty straight but it wasn't long. It became more narrow and twisty. Not only that, but they were constantly going uphill. At one point Andy had to pull over to the side of the road to let another car going the opposite direction cross the narrow bridge before they could proceed. The rest of the road was uphill till they finally got to the top of the mountain. At the top they came to a building that had a large sign across the entrance way. It said;

HALEAKALA VISTOR CENTER
(House of the Sun) Elevation 9,740 feet

Andy and Tina walked through the visitor center enjoying the displays. Next they took the path up to the highest point. A sign there told them that they were at an elevation of 10,023 feet. From there they could see about six large craters.

"My goodness," said Tina in awe. "It's like I'm looking down on the crater of the moon."

"That is a great description," said Andy. "You should be a writer. I have never been on the moon but I can see what you mean." They continued walking around the path taking in the view from different locations. They spent nearly an hour enjoying the spectacular views of the craters.

"Tina," said Andy. "I know that we probably will never be able to come here again, but we had better leave. It is now eleven thirty. It will take us over two hours to get home. I think we should leave go to the condo have lunch and then relax and enjoy the condo.

"I have taken plenty of pictures. Every time I will look at them I'll be reliving the trip." They finally left. Andy was right. It took almost two hours to get back. They got back to the condo a little before two o'clock. They had lunch and then after relaxing for a while they went swimming in the ocean at the end of the condo's back yard. In the water they became children again. They splashed water on each other, then, they chased each other around the water trying to get even from the last trick. She would swim away and then come back under water and grabbing Andy's feet try to lift dump him head first in the water. They continued playing for about an hour. Then it happened. Tina had splash water in Andy's face Andy chased after her. She ran towards the shore. Andy grabbed her shoulder causing her to turn around and fall on her back on the sand. Andy fell on top of her. They ended up face to face. Their lips were less than an inch apart. Andy lost control. He pressed his lips on hers. The passion he felt was something he had never felt before. He then put his arms around her and pulled her body up tight next to his. He pressed his lips tighter on hers. He felt a chill run down his spine. Tina didn't move. They held the kiss for a long passionate time. Andy wasn't thinking at all. He just enjoyed the feeling that was completely new to him. Then suddenly he snapped out of it. What was he doing, he asked himself. He pulled himself away from Tina. For a moment they just stared into each other's eyes. Andy thought he saw passion in her face. It only lasted for a few seconds. Then Tina pulled herself up and away from Andy.

"What are you doing," she asked in a state of shock?

"I'm sorry," said Andy. He was in a state of confusion. "I was having so much fun and enjoyed your company so much that I lost control."

"I think we should go back to oahu," said Tina. "I would like to spend the next days under an umbrella at the Hotel outrigger before I have to leave"

"Don't you want to stay here and relax for a day," asked Andy. "No," said Tina. "I want to go back first thing in the morning." "Look Tina," said Andy. "I'm sorry. I lost control. I know I broke the trust you had in me. We are best friends. Is it wrong for good friends to kiss?"

"I don't know," said Tina. "I can't think straight right now." "Look," begged Andy. "I'm sorry. Can't you forgive me this once? Please don't be angry with me."

"Oh Andy," said Tina. "I'm not angry with you. Please take me back to the hotel. I have some thinking to do." The rest of the evening they both sat on the porch and relaxed. Not much was said after that.

The next morning they caught the first flight back to oahu. They arrived at the Honolulu Airport at ten thirty. Andy rented a car and the drove to the outrigger Hotel.

"Listen," said Tina. "I want to go up take a shower and come down for lunch. I'll meet you here at the lobby. We can go in and have lunch together. I have been doing a lot of thinking. We have to talk." Andy was glad to hear her said that. Perhaps she decided to forgive and forget. She seemed to be almost back to her jolly self. Andy went up, took a shower, got cleaned up and went down to the lobby. They got there at the same time. It was like it was planned. They were about to leave the lobby when they heard a loud voice call out.

"Christina" Tina turned around and began walking toward the man who had call out her name.

"Paul," she said. "What are you doing here"? Paul didn't answer. He just grabbed her, wrapped his arms around her, and gave her a passionate kiss. Tina responded by putting her arms around his neck. Andy felt a pain in his chest. He felt like his heart stopped. He suddenly realized that he had fallen deeply in love with her. He noticed that Paul was a slim, tall and a very handsome man. He was very elegantly dressed. Andy felt that he could never compete with him. At that moment he made up his mind. He decided that he could not stay there and watch Tina and Paul enjoy their time together. He headed up to his room and packed his suitcases. He had to leave right away.

Down in the lobby, Tina grabbed Paul by the arm and pulled him into the lounge.

"We have to talk," Tina said as she brought him to a couch in the lounge and asked him to sit down. "We have to talk," she repeated. "I actually came here because I felt I needed a lot of time to think. I was sure you would never show up. You being here is the surprise of my life."

"It was that obvious that I didn't want to come here," said Paul. "To be honest with you I have to admit that my having important business to attend to was an excuse. You know that I hate being here in the boondocks. As a matter of facts I was hoping that I could convince you to leave early, like tomorrow."

"That's the point," said Tina. "We both like different things. For example, you are hoping that you will get a partnership and move to New York. The very thought of living in New York drives me crazy. I am a small town girl. I could never live in New York or any big town.

"I was hoping that I could change you," said Paul.

"That is the other point I want to bring up," said Tina. "I think you are a very handsome man. You are a very intelligent man. You are a good catch for a woman. That is what I feel for you. It is respect and the feeling that I have made a great catch. But you see that is not love. I don't think that you love me either. You don't love me for what I really am but what you want to change me into."

"So what are you saying," asked Paul?"

"I'm saying that if we got married that in a few years we would go back to our real selves and hate each other. Paul you are a great guy and someone will be very lucky to get you but it isn't me." Tina then removed her engagement ring and handed it to Paul.

"I'm so sorry Paul. I have enjoyed the three years we have spent together."

"Then I am leaving here right now," said Paul. "I hate every minute that I am here. I'm not even going to check in. goodbye Christina." He then grabbed his suitcase and left. Tina felt relieved. She realized that the kiss that Paul gave her a little while ago told her all that she needed to know. That kiss did nothing to her. She then remembered the kiss Andy gave her at the condo. It had given her a thrill she had never felt before. Her spine still tingles from that kiss. She now fully realizes that she was madly in love with Andy. She realized that she had been in love with him from the beginning. She wondered why it took her so long to realize it. Tina then went into the lobby hoping that Andy was still there. He wasn't. She then went into the restaurant. She thought maybe he went in to have lunch thinking that she was going to have lunch with Paul. She looked all around but he wasn't there. She wondered where he could be. Then she wondered if he had gone down to the beach. They had planned to go there after lunch. She walked across the beach in front of all the umbrellas to see if he was there. He was not anywhere in the area. She went back to the lobby. Perhaps he was discouraged seeing her with Paul and went back to his room. Tina was now sure that Andy loved her as she loved him. She decided to call his room. going up to the registration desk she asked the young man standing there.

"Can you give me the phone number of Andrew Brown's room," she asked. The young man looked it up in the computer but could not find it. Just then the regular attendant can in from the back room.

"Hi," she said. "Are you looking for Andrew Brown?" "I would like his room phone number," asked Tina.

"You just missed him the attendant answered. "He just checked out. He checked out less than five minutes ago. If you run out front he may still be there waiting for a cab." Tina knew that Andy had a rented car. But she knew where he parked it last night when they got home. She ran out to the parking lot but the car was gone. She checked her purse to see if she had enough money to pay a cab fare to the airport. She did. Fortunately a cab was just dropping off a young couple. She got into the cab.

"Please take me to the airport as soon as you can," Tina asked. The driver took off immediately. When they got to the airport Tina paid the cab fare and hurried into the airport. She looked around. She did not see Andy or Paul. She went to the flight clerk.

"When is the flight to LA departing," she asked.

"You just missed it," said the clerk. "The next one will leave at nine fifteen tonight."

"When is the flight to San Francisco leaving?

"The last one left about fifteen minutes ago," said the clerk. The next on will not leave until eight tomorrow morning."

"Thank you," said Tina. "I will have to think about this." Tina was so down hearted that she couldn't think straight. She left and took a cab back to the hotel. At the hotel she decided that she could not spend the next two days alone without Andy. She decided to leave on the nine thirty flight to LA. She called and made reservations, packed and was ready to leave. She was so depressed that she couldn't eat lunch. She decided to just go to the airport and wait there for her flight. She packed and got a cab to the airport. She decided at about eight that she had better get something to eat. She hadn't had anything since that morning. She found a little area in the airport that served burgers. She had one and headed back to the waiting area.

The plane landed in LA early the next morning. Tina grabbed a cab and went to the closest hotel for the night. The next morning she slept till nine, got dressed, and went down for breakfast. She was feeling a little better so she sat with a cup of coffee and thought about how she was going to find Andy. Suddenly it dawned on her that she didn't even know what state he was from. When she got to the airport to return to her home, she saw a rack with telephone books on it from many large cities. She looked through a couple in the hopes that she would miraculously find Andy's number. She was not surprised to find that there were two pages of people named Brown in each book. Later that day she called her friend Betty, telling her that she was coming home. She then took the flight that took her home.

She landed in Cleveland at six fifteen. While she was retrieving her luggage she heard her name called. She turned around to see who was calling her. It was her best friend Betty.

"Betty," said Tina. "What are you doing here?" "I come to drive you home," answered Betty. "How did you know I was coming home?"

"You told me yesterday that you were coming home," said Betty. "I checked all the flight and I found that this was the only flight that you could have been on."

"You are god sent," said Tina. on the way home Betty turned to Tina.

"Alright now," she started. "Tell me what is going on." "Nothing is going on," answered Tina. "What makes you think there is?"

"Come now," said Betty. "I'm your best friend. We have known each other since college. I know you better than I know myself. When you called from Hawaii, not only did I notice that you were coming home early, but I could tell from your voice that you were depressed. And look at you now. You are not the upbeat, happy go lucky girl I knew and loved. What happened in Hawaii that has done this to you?" Tina then related to Betty all that she and Andy did in Hawaii. She told her about the trip to Kauai. She told her about flying over the grand Canyon of the Pacific. She told her about the trip to the Big Island. How she had walked on the hot lava rock. She related the final trip to maui and how they look down on the craters. She then told her about the last hours at the Palms Condo at maui. Tina told Betty that the condo was like paradise.

"That sound great," said Betty. "So why does that make you so sad?"

"It's what happened the last hour at the condo," said Tina. "ok," said Betty. "Come on tell me what happened."

"We were swimming down in the ocean. The condo was located by the ocean. We were having fun when I playfully splashed him with water. He tried to get even so I ran toward the shore. He caught up to me and as I turned he fell on top of me. When we landed on the beach his lips were about an inch from mine. Suddenly he kissed me. Betty, I have never felt anything like that in my whole life. I had butterflies in my belly. I had a chill go down my spine. I was in such a state of confusion that I asked to leave and go back to the hotel we originally had in oahu"

"So you actually fell in love with Andy," asked Betty?

"I didn't know it at the time. I had never felt that way before. I didn't know what real love was like."

"What about Paul," asked Betty? "In two week he couldn't show up for a few days?"

"He did show up Thursday to ask me to go home early," said Tina. "We were ready to go to lunch when

Paul showed up. That is what caused all the problems. Paul grabbed me and kissed me hard on the lips. That's when I realized that I was in love with Andy. The kiss I had with Paul was like kissing a stone statue. So I asked him to go into the lounge and sit down. I explained to him that he was a fantastic person. I told him that he was intelligent and very handsome and I was going with him because he was a good catch. I told him that was not enough that I didn't really love him. So I gave him back his ring."

"You have no Idea how happy that makes me," said Betty. "I never liked him. He was too arrogant. He was high society compared to us. So what happened to Andy?"

"After I parted with Paul I went looking for Andy to tell him that I loved him. I couldn't find him. He disappeared. I asked the hotel clerk and she told me the Andy had checked out five minutes earlier. I think seeing Paul and I together did him in. I even went to the airport but it was too late."

"It seems that he loves you too," said Betty. "We will find him. Do you know where he lives?"

"That is the problem," said Tina. "I don't even know what state he lives in."

"What do you know about him," asked Betty?

"All I know is that he is an electronic professor at a university. I don't know what university. All I remember is that the city he lives in has something green it the name."

"That's alright," said Betty. "What is his last name?" "His name is Andrew J Brown," said Tina.

"Wow," said Betty. "That does make it more difficult. I'm sure there are three pages of Browns in every phone book." When they got home Tina carried her suitcase inside. Betty went with her.

"Do you want to go out to eat," asked Tina?

"We have little time before we eat," said Betty. "Let's get on your computer and see if we can find your Andy. I can't stand seeing you so sad."

"I appreciate your efforts," said Tina with a very sad smile. They spent the next two hours on the computer with no results.

"Let's go out to eat," said Betty. "oh my, I almost forget. I made a special dinner at my house for you. I think we will have to warm it up before we can eat it. Anyway, don't worry. I promise that I will never give up helping you find your true love. Besides, I'm sure he will be looking for you when he realizes that he can't live without you."

"I don't think so," said Tina. "He thinks that Paul and I are still planning to get married."

Betty kept her word. The next day she got together with Tina and ran all that they knew through the computer. They had no success.

"You know Tina," said Betty. "We have only one choice. We have to take one state at a time and find all the colleges in that state and then check each college to see if an Andrew Brown teaches there."

"Sounds like lot of work," said Tina. "But I don't think I have any other choice. However, I don't want to put that load on your shoulder. I will take care of it all myself."

Sure," said Betty. "You will find him when you retire. I promised that I will never give up. However let's do it this way. I will take the Eastern States and you take the Western States."

"I hate to do that to you but I need to find Andy soon or I will die. ok let's start tomorrow."

They did that for the next two months. They found that the average number of colleges in each state was four. Some had only two some had five. Checking one university every night, with some nights off, averaged about a week for each state. By the time school started in September they covered only ten states. After school started, they could only work on it on weekends. It was near the end of october that Tina was ready to give up. one Saturday after lunch, when they got together to continue checking colleges, Tina put her hand on Betty's hand.

"Listen Betty," she said. "I appreciate the effort that you have put into finding Andy. But this effort has gotten out of hand. I have prayed to god five times every day. I think we should have faith in god. We are trying to do this job ourselves. We should trust god. If Andy and I are to be together let god find him. We are doing the same sin that the king of Israel did when they went to Egypt for help instead of asking god."

"Alright," said Betty. "Let's pray together." Betty grabbed Tina's hand and prayed. "Dear Lord, forgive us for forgetting you. Please find Andy for Tina."

"Thank you," said Tina "You are a fantastic friend."

"I have an idea," said Betty. "It is about two o'clock. I have wanted to go to Summit mall. They have a special sale on clothes. They are trying get rid of their summer stock. Come with me. It will give us a little free time. It will give us something else to think about." "I don't think so," said Tina. "I have plenty of school work to think about."

"I insist. I could use the company. You can give me your opinion on things I want to buy."

"Since you put it that way," said Tina. "Let's go." After Tina change into better clothes, they left. They spent about two hours looking at different items. Betty ended up buying two dresses and a pair of shoes. It was getting close to six when Betty suggested they go to the restaurant at the entrance of the mall. As they walked inside the mall Tina suddenly stopped.

"What's the matter," asked Betty?

"It's so strange," said Tina. "See that fellow look-ing into that shop window. It's amazing how much he looks like Andy."

"That is a normal," said Betty. "Every slim, tall, and handsome man is going to remind you of Andy." The man was slightly turned the other way looking in the store window. His face was looking away from Betty and Tina. At that moment the fellow turned and started to walk toward them. Tina let out a yell.

"Andy," she yelled. She then ran up to the man and threw her arms around him.

"Tina," said Andy. "What are you doing here?" "I'm shopping with my best friend," said Tina.

"No, I mean here in ohio," said Andy looking around. "Is Paul here with you? Did you get married before school started?"

"You know Andy," she said with a smile on her face. "For a very intelligent man you can be such an idiot."

"So I am an Idiot," said Andy.

"Yes," said Tina hugging him again. "If you had waited and not run away you would have learned something."

"What great knowledge would I have learn?" asked Andy having no idea of what she was talking about.

"You would have learned how much I love you," said Tina with love in her voice. Andy looked stunned.

"I saw you give Paul a passionate kiss," said Andy. "I couldn't stay and watch you and Paul together. I had to leave. What happened after I left? What did I miss?"

"I took Paul by the hand and brought him into the lounge and sat him down. I explained that I admired him and cared a great deal for him but that I didn't love him. Then I gave him back his ring and went look-ing for you to tell you how much I love you."

"I'm so sorry," said Andy "I had no idea. I thought I had lost you. When I saw the passionate kiss you had with Paul I thought my heart stopped. I should have told you how much I love you."

"That kiss from Paul told me how much I loved you," said Tina. "That kiss was like I put my lips on a clay statue."

"You will never believe how much I have suffered these last four months," said Andy. "If you loved me so much why haven't you contacted me?"

"Where would I have contacted you? I don't even know what state you live in. Betty and I have worked every day trying to find you. All I knew is that you taught electronics at a university. Betty and I have been calling all the universities. To date we have covered twelve states. It has taken us four months to do that. Speaking of Betty, I want you to meet my best friend. I'm sorry Betty I didn't mean to ignore you. This is Andy."

"Hi Andy," said Betty. "I have heard so much about you I feel I know you. I'm almost in love with you too."

"It's nice to meet you too," said Andy. "It's nice to be loved." "Listen lovers," said Betty. "You two have a lot to talk about and I would guess a lot of planning to do. So I would like to leave you two. Do you think you can find a way home Tina?"

"Don't worry about that," said Andy. "I will see her home. I hope we will be seeing a lot of you."

"You will get tired of seeing me," said Betty with laughter. "good bye for now."

"Good bye," said Tina and Andy together. After Betty left Andy turned to Tina.

"You know, you didn't answer my question. What are you doing here in ohio? Are you visiting a relative? It is such a coincidence that we should meet this way."

"I live here," said Tina. "I live in Copley. I am a teacher at Copley High School. Where are you from?"

"I live here in Fairlawn,"said Andy. "I teach electronics at Akron University. I live a walking distance from here. Copley High School is about a ten minutes from my house."

"And I have been looking all over the US for you," said Tina, "and here we are neighbors."

"Let's go to Red Lobster," said Andy. "We have a lot of planning to do.

"Ok," said Tina. "We can't do much hugging and kissing here which is what I would prefer." They left the mall and were soon sitting at Red Lobster ordering their dinner.

"I am never letting you out of my sight. I want to spend the rest of my life with you," said Andy.

"Is that a proposal?" asked Tina with a smile on her face. "It's more like a pre-proposal," answered Andy.

"Why a pre-proposal," asked Tina?

"Because it isn't official until I give you a ring," said Andy. "Sorry, I don't have ring yet."

"So what is the plan," asked Tina?

"That is what we are here to talk about," said Andy. They decided to remain there drinking coffee while they thought of what to do next.

"First I will go to my jewelry shop and get you a ring," started Andy. "Then, we will determine where we are going to live and where we are going to get married."

"I would like to suggest that we live in the house you designed and built," suggested Tina. "Since we will live in your home we should get married at the church you belong." Andy was delighted that they had that settled. The rest of the evening they discussed the wedding date, the hall where they will celebrate the wedding, and of course where they will spend their honeymoon. They had no problem. They decided that some of the answers would be answered after they speak to the church pastor and the hall where they both thought they would like to celebrate. By the time they had discussed everything it got pretty late.

"I had better take you home," said Andy. "It is getting late." "Before you take me home I would like to see the home I am going to live in," suggested Tina. "It's not really that late. Andy agreed and drove to his house. As he pulled into the garage, Tina moved on his seat in the car and after Andy turned the engine off she wrapped her arms around him and started to kiss him. Tina never saw the house that night. Actually they never got out of the car.

The End

www.ingramcontent.com/pod-product-compliance
Lightning Source LLC
Chambersburg PA
CBHW031242210726
48287CB00003B/863